DREAMS

P A WILSON

Free eBook

Claim your copy of Buying Into Death when you use the QR code to sign up for my newsletter and follow Charity as she solves her fastest case yet!

Chapter 1

"Hey, Charity, are you around?" Val's voice floated up to the patio.

I'd given up trying to make her knock on the door like a normal person and handed her a key. That way I didn't waste energy wondering how she broke in. It's not like she was disturbing anything private in my life anyway.

"Grab a coke and come up," I said. The great thing about a tiny home is you don't need to yell. Or maybe it's just my neighborhood, where yelling gets you the wrong kind of attention.

I heard the fridge slam and then Val appeared in the door to the patio, Rory right behind her. They stepped out and grabbed a plastic chair each. I put the printout from my only actually active case face down on the table and dropped my phone on it as a paperweight.

"What are you doing?" Val asked.

She'd learned to preface her requests for favors with what appeared to be concern for other people. I looked forward to when she finally exited the self-centered teenage phase. Her history delayed her maturity but hadn't made her jaded, which was good — in the long term.

"Preparing for a case." I pushed the bowl of chips toward them. "Are you just visiting?"

"Lu and Matthieu left today, right?"

My best friend and her husband were spending the next three months in France. At least I hoped it was only that long.

"Yes," I said. "We had dinner yesterday. I've been lectured about making friends while she was gone." Seriously, you'd think I didn't know how to do those things.

"She's such a mom. Are you busy with more than that case?" She nodded toward the file.

"We winnowed the outstanding cases down," I said. "I'll be looking for more clients soon."

Val ran her own business, so she knew how hard it might be to find new clients. The personal organization consultant, as she called it, morphed occasionally as she found new interests. Currently she was working with Rory's dad to create order in their archived files.

Rory MacDonald was the only child of Vancouver's most famous and successful lawyer, Rance MacDonald. He didn't want to follow his dad's path and was trying his hand at being a documentary movie auteur. Rance had done me a few favors too, and maybe he had some cases to refer to me. It would give me something to fill my time.

"I thought maybe you wanted to go out for dinner," Val said.

Hmm, that was a first. "Lu told you to make sure I didn't spend the entire time moping?"

"Yes," Rory said. "But that's not the only reason."

"I was going to tell her our idea over dinner," Val said.

"We'll still go," Rory said. He turned to me and straightened up, going from casual semi-hipster to professional as he did. I wondered if his dad gave him some pointers.

"Charity," he said. "I, we, I mean. We were thinking about how to help you keep busy. I know you don't have much work going on and we didn't want to find you moping, that part is true."

I held up my hand to stop him. "Rory, you've got the body language down, but you need to be more focused when you talk if you want to be taken seriously."

He asked me a while back to do that. Give him feedback without sugar coating it. We shared that facet of personality. We didn't recognize hints about ourselves. We needed it blunt.

He nodded and then closed his eyes for a moment. "Thanks. I think it would do us both some good if I started following you around and filming your investigations."

"No." He couldn't be with me all the time. How would I sneak off for an afternoon of binging TV?

Val groaned. "You didn't even think about it."

"Clients won't like it. I might get sued if they see their case on the screen. I have to go into some iffy situations that would be worse if Rory were there. Informants wouldn't talk if they were on camera. Is that enough thought?"

Rory touched Val's arm to stop her from speaking again.

"All very good objections," he said. "But I would only film when we had permission. Maybe your clients would like having a visual of the investigations."

"Maybe they would, but I don't want them to learn what I do to close a case."

"I could edit out what you don't want them to see."

While Rory and I talked, Val pouted and watched the seagulls. I imagined the discussion before they came. Rory telling Val not to use emotional blackmail to get her way; Val saying I should just do what she asked. I had to give the guy credit. He would probably be a success in the film world with lots of persistence. But he thought we were still negotiating, and I planned to stand firm.

That said, I knew how to end this kind of thing. "Let me think about it."

"That's all I ask."

Now that I'd won, even though Rory thought he was still in the game, I could be magnanimous. "Where do you want to go for dinner? My treat."

It turned out the dinner was just an excuse. Rory said he had things to do and left Val with me. If I didn't know him better, I would have sworn he was sulking, but that's not how Rory did things. At a wild guess, I imagined he was off thinking of a new avenue to convince me to agree.

Val offered to make something, but I ordered pizza.

"Why don't we stay up here until it arrives?" Val asked. "It's a nice day, and you look like you could use the relaxation."

"What's the other favor?" I asked.

"Nothing. I'm just worried about you."

There was actual sincerity in her voice. Maybe she was growing up. "I'm over Jake."

"But you haven't met anyone new. You're not even trying. You aren't moving on."

I picked up my notes and started for the door. "I didn't say I was ready to date. I'm too busy with work."

Val rolled her eyes.

"Don't start with me, Val. I'll date when I'm ready. With Lu and Matthieu heading to France, I'm going to be busy with clients."

Downstairs, I dropped the papers on the counter and grabbed a beer for me and another soda for Val.

"Matthieu said you didn't have much work."

Matthieu had a big mouth. "I'll get new ones."

"Well, maybe you could come out with us some time and maybe you'll meet someone."

"I don't think I'll find someone suitable for me by hanging out with you." I turned on the TV, hoping it would end the conversation.

"What about hanging with someone your age?" Val plopped onto the sofa beside me.

"I don't know anyone like that." I had a very small circle of friends. Two. One was on her way to France, the other was on my sofa.

Val grabbed the remote. "What about Leigh?"

"We're not friends." I appreciated her help and her ability to save my life more than once, but I was sure Leigh wouldn't think of me as a friend either.

Val stopped flicking the channels and settled on a reality show. "Try asking. Or I can invite you both over for dinner and you could get to know her better and then suggest you go to a bar or something."

"Now it sounds like you're setting us up," I said. "Just watch the show."

"Fine."

We sat unspeaking for the twenty minutes it took for the pizza to arrive. I let the guy through the security gate and met him halfway down the finger dock to pay him. Usually I waited for deliveries at my door. Tonight, I figured Val would try to set me up with him if I let him any closer.

When I got back, the show was finishing, and the news starting. Val had put plates and napkins on the coffee table.

"Let's check out a movie," she said, pulling a slice from the box.

"I want the news."

"You can watch it online. You don't have to wait for them to feed stuff to you."

If I did that, I would be too close to Facebook and Twitter. I didn't want to admit that to Val. "Let's just hear what they have to say and then we can stream a movie."

Val laughed and sat back, chewing on her pizza.

I wanted to hear if the cops had made any progress on the murder of a journalist. She fell down a staircase at the hospital. Going to the most dangerous parts of the world to get a story makes you careful, so I had a hard time believing she fell by accident. If they didn't have some kind of lead by now, it might be a hard case to solve.

"It is unclear what Ms. LaSalle was doing at the hospital," the male anchor said. "Our sources have been unable to identify any family or friends who had been admitted. The police are asking for anyone who may have seen her while at the hospital to contact them with any information. "

As usual on this channel, the other anchor needed to chip in part of the story. I guess we were supposed to think they'd done a joint investigation.

"Bob, do we know if the police contacted her employer?"

"They are refusing to give a statement," Bob answered. "It is possible that she was there in a freelance capacity."

The female anchor smiled. "I'm sure we'll have more information soon." She turned to face the camera and the image behind her changed to show a car wreck. "An accident southbound on the Oak Street Bridge delayed the commute by several hours tonight."

"It would be great if you had a case like that," Val said. "I mean, not great that someone got murdered. If Rory could document a murder case, he'd be famous right away."

"Only the cops investigate murders. Don't bother to ask, there's no way they would agree. And I won't agree to let Rory follow me around."

Val decided she'd rather spend the rest of the evening with Rory and called a cab as soon as the last slice of pizza disappeared. It gave me free time; time I should be spending on the employee espionage case, but sorting through telephone records and emails didn't appear on my list of things I wanted to do; binging a show did.

Before I found the one I wanted, my phone rang. For someone who apparently had no friends and no life, I sure had a lot of interruptions.

"Hi, Leigh," I said after checking the caller ID.

"Hey, Charity." She sounded overly cheerful. When Leigh, the police officer, called, it was more often a warning to stay away from something or a scolding for having done something. I didn't think Leigh the police detective would be much different. "Listen, I called because I heard you're at loose ends right now. I thought we could go out for a drink sometime. Maybe tomorrow?"

I sighed. "Who put you up to managing my social life?"

"Busted. Let's hope I'm better at lying to suspects than I am to anyone else. Lu said you might turn into a hermit."

Would that be bad?

"Why won't they let me be? I have recovered from breakups before."

"I don't know you that well, but if I had to guess, this one is different. I didn't even know you had a boyfriend. But since he ended it, you haven't bothered me for help, or needed me to get you out of a jam."

If even Leigh could see there was a problem, maybe I was in denial. Then again, maybe I was only being independent.

"For the record, I ended it." Not exactly the truth, but I felt better with the lie. "Okay, drinks tomorrow. Where?"

"You know Pourhouse down on Water?" she asked.

"At seven?"

"Good enough. I have an opportunity you might be interested in."

It wasn't that late, and I didn't want to wait until tomorrow. "How about in an hour instead?"

Leigh hesitated and that got me worried. "Okay, I'll make some arrangements. See you there."

Arrangements? Was this some kind of trap? Had I crossed a line lately? If the cops wanted me, they knew where I lived. I know, paranoia is not a great character trait, at least not when I'm between cases.

I was wearing jeans and an old sweatshirt since the only thing I planned was a night at home. I briefly considered not changing, but realized I'd end up being more uncomfortable than if I wore something more appropriate. After all, if Leigh needed to 'make arrangements' then I could make an effort.

A quick shower, some dressier black pants and green silk tank under a sheer pullover made me look like I might be worthy of a date. I didn't do full makeup, but a bit of blush, mascara, and lipstick helped me look alive.

I hated to admit it, but getting ready made me feel some enthusiasm for the event. I called a taxi because I didn't want to spoil the effect by walking the twenty minutes to the bar.

Chapter 2

Leigh got out of a cab across the street just as mine pulled away. Without her cop look, she looked five years younger. Her blond hair was loose around her face, she wore makeup too, and her clothes flattered rather than tried to hide her athletic body. Maybe I needed a few lessons on how to dress. Was it weird that I felt a flash of jealousy because guys might not notice me with her around? *Yes.*

I waved and waited for her to cross the street before heading in. The bar was half empty and lacked the desperation I remembered from the last time I hung around one at almost eleven at night.

We found a table and ordered drinks. "So, an opportunity?" I didn't want to waste time dancing around the information.

"Relax," Leigh said. "Let me start at the beginning."

"Yeah. Always the best place to start," Val said as she pulled out a chair and joined us.

"I thought you went home to Rory."

"Really? I thought you were a detective. You are so

easy to lie to, Charity. I'm here because I don't trust you to listen."

Leigh called the waiter over and Val ordered a soda.

"That was my idea," Leigh said. "It's important to me, and I thought Val could help."

Everything she said sounded like proof people were ganging up on me. I could have stayed home on my couch for this. "Start talking. I actually looked forward to a night out, so your opportunity better be good."

Val and Leigh exchanged glances.

"You know I've been promoted," Leigh said.

"Yeah, to detective," I said.

"Well, it's not what I hoped. Don't get me wrong, the work is great, I just wish I got access to the important cases."

"So, you want to join our agency?" I would miss her as an asset on the force, but Leigh would bring experience to our team I didn't have, and connections Matthieu was still trying to make.

"No," Leigh said. She waved her hands as if wiping out the idea. "I like being a cop. Today, my boss offered to let me be in charge of some old cases — not cold exactly, but stalled."

"Congrats," I said. "We'll celebrate."

"No, just listen, Charity," Val said.

"You heard about that journalist, right?" Leigh said. "Well, we're under a lot of pressure to solve her murder, so most of the guys are assigned to her case. We're short staffed right now and these cases aren't low enough priority to be set aside."

"I still don't understand why I'm here." I didn't know her well, but Leigh hadn't struck me as the type to brag.

"She needs help and there aren't any other cops, or

maybe they don't want to help." Val looked at Leigh as she said the last bit.

"It's not like that. I need to prove myself before I'm allowed to join the club, but no one would jeopardize a case to keep me out."

I agreed with Leigh, mostly from experience. The cops were mad at me for a while, but they still did their job. Helping me out wasn't part of the job. Cooperation came as a benefit from a relationship. I was currently working on that.

"Still don't get it," I said. Although I had an idea, I couldn't believe I would be sanctioned to help.

"I got a budget to hire a contractor," Leigh said. "I also got the okay for you to be that contractor. Unless you're too busy."

I sipped my drink to give my mouth something to do that didn't include blurting out my first thought: a solid no. Some part of my brain mentioned that I could finish the outstanding case in a few hours of detecting. The voice also reminded me that with nothing to do, I might just sit around eating and getting fat.

"You're bored, Charity," Val said, misinterpreting my silence. "You need to do something, and if it's not this, I'll start setting you up with dates and mess around in your love life."

I put down my glass. "Here's the deal. I'll help, but if there's any game-playing from the official side, I'm not holding back. Are you okay with my conditions, Leigh?"

"I prefer you not trash my career, but I don't see any way of stopping you." She looked at her watch. "I have to go. I'll see you at eight thirty tomorrow in my cubicle?"

I gave a thumbs up and Leigh left us.

"Val, you don't need to take care of me," I said.

"You say that, but you aren't doing anything to reassure us you're okay." She finished her soda and stood. "I gotta go, you should too. Get a good night's sleep and make an impression tomorrow. A good one!"

I DIDN'T OBEY VAL. I spent most of the night closing out my case and writing the report for the client. I'd give it another look over when I got home later and send it off. But I wanted to look like I fit in an office full of cops, so I needed a little sleep, a shower, and more than a little makeup for that to happen.

I met Leigh in the reception area of the police station on Cambie. It wasn't as convenient as the one on Main, but the homicide department had moved and so I wouldn't be walking to work much. This time instead of being escorted back to Leigh's desk, I filled out a form and was rewarded with a visitor badge. Until someone revoked it, I could access the station without escort at any time. I tried not to think of ways I would screw up, but all that documentation on criminals sang welcome to me as soon as the badge hung around my neck.

"Charity," Leigh said in a tone that told me she'd called me more than once. "You'll get a spare cube later, but we can start right now."

I followed her back to the bullpen, making note as she pointed out the lunchroom, bathroom, and file room.

"Will I get access to the system?"

"Visitor access," Leigh said. "Same as the file room. You won't be able to alter anything on a document, but you can look at anything that isn't classified. You can review anything in the room but won't be able to take anything out."

I didn't know if I was more disappointed I couldn't run

wild and free through the police records, or relieved they had good control. "So, three cases," I said.

Leigh picked up the top file. "The oldest first. Jackson Tripton, dead by poison May 3 this year. No lover on the side, no real enemies. We cleared the wife, although she remarried only six weeks later."

"You mean no known enemies," I said. "How did you clear the wife?"

"Alibi. I know what you're going to say, but she didn't leave the poison for him to take while she had an alibi. We found an injection mark on his foot."

I thought that sounded a little too pat, but accusing the cops of being facile with a case was not the way to start out our working relationship. "Okay. Do I get a copy of the file?"

"Just don't take anything out of the office," she said, handing me the folder. "Next, we have Alex Sandhu, stabbed May 6. It looks like he was taking a morning run, and someone saw him as an easy target."

She lay the file open in front of me, the pictures were first. "Someone was angry," I said. The autopsy photo showed five wounds around his heart. "How far did you get?"

"It does look personal," Leigh said. "The investigating officer didn't make any progress. No witnesses. It was early in the morning. The knife was gone, and we only found his DNA."

These both seemed more than stale. It sounded to me like they were on the back burner from day one. "And the last one?"

"Mary Copp, not murder, yet. She was pushed off the seawall on May 17. A cyclist saw the attack and called 911. Copp is in VGH in a coma. We're hoping she'll tell us something if she comes out of it."

"The cyclist?"

"Didn't see enough detail. Only that it was definitely not an accident. The suspect is medium build, but wearing sweats and a hoodie, so he's not sure if the attacker was male or female."

"How come I haven't heard of these?" It wasn't like we were the murder capital of Canada. We still cared enough to report on deaths like this.

"They were on the news, but it was around the time of the election. All three were bumped off the front page by the stories discrediting one or the other candidate."

I checked the dates on the file. All within three weeks. Not regular spacing, the first two in the first week of May, the last right after the election was over. "Is that unusual? To have them close together?"

"Yes. We don't get many murders, but don't make a conspiracy case out of it. The brass won't appreciate you trying to sensationalize the cases."

"If conspiracy is there, we'll find it," I said. "So, what do we do first?"

It was a boring day. Leigh made me dig into the files and learn all the facts before she would even listen to an idea of how to proceed. By the end of the day, I knew everything and maybe tomorrow we could get some interviews down.

I SAT in the bar at the Bayshore waiting for Leigh to return from the bathroom. Our drink orders were on their way. That was the second bonus of working with Leigh, she liked to end the day with a bit of socializing. Matthieu and I mostly worked independently and, looking back, maybe that helped me turn into a hermit.

"Hey," Val's voice came from behind me.

I turned, and she walked up with Rory and grabbed a chair to join us. "How did you know I was here?" It wasn't like Val to just drop into a bar...or at least I didn't think so.

"I called them," Leigh said, sliding into her chair.

This was starting to feel like a set up. "Why?" I tried not to sound suspicious, but I didn't like feeling maneuvered.

Leigh took her drink from the waiter. "We've been given orders."

"You weren't supposed to tell her," Val said, slumping into the chair.

"Babe, Charity's not stupid. She already figured it out." Rory ordered two sodas and sat back in the chair like he was observing a scene from a movie.

That last night at dinner, Lu had been anxious, but I thought I'd settled her mind. When she fell in love with Matthieu, I asked her not to move to France and leave me alone. When they stayed here, I said it was a joke, and it was — mostly.

"She's supposed to be thinking about herself, not worrying about me." If I ruined their extended vacation, I'd never forgive myself.

"She is," Leigh said. "That's why we agreed to keep you occupied."

"Yeah, that and you need to find something more interesting than the TV. You aren't getting younger," Val said.

I didn't respond to the comment; she was young enough that I might seem ancient. If she was trying to get a rise out of me, I wouldn't give her the satisfaction.

"Do you really need help on the cases? Or is this in aid of project Stop Charity Moping?"

"That is real," Leigh said. "I wouldn't risk my career by involving a civilian without approval. That said, I fought for you to be the consultant because you are a good investigator."

"What cases?" Val asked.

"We can't talk about them," I said before Leigh could.

"Three possible murders," Leigh said before I finished. "Or I guess, two possible murders and a definite attempted."

Val nudged Rory.

He slid a glance at me, his face flushing. "Would it help to have the investigation documented?"

Now I got the real setup. Val was going to push this until she got her way. Fortunately, this wasn't for me to shut down. Leigh could drop the official line and that would be the end.

"What do you mean?" she asked.

"So, you know I'm a documentary filmmaker," Rory said, his face losing the embarrassed flush as he got excited about his dream. "The real crime stuff is hot now. I could film you in your investigation and then edit it into a short each day for my YouTube channel."

Leigh nodded for him to continue.

"Then I'd take the highlights and create a cut for festival entries...Sundance and stuff."

"I can't authorize that," Leigh said.

"Why not?" Val asked.

"Babe," Rory said.

"Let me finish," Leigh said. "You need to learn to listen better if you want to get ahead in any business. I said *I* couldn't authorize it, but I can pass the request to my boss. If you can live with whatever restrictions she lays out?"

Val sat up. "What kind of restrictions? Rory can't sacrifice his art for some stupid rules."

I hid my smile by taking a drink. Val looked like she'd taken over as Rory's manager. He needed someone to be pushy for him. In my mind he was too willing to take the first answer. I knew about the film industry from being Jake's girlfriend. There was a no, and there was an absolutely not. You got the yes somewhere between the two.

"I'll find out. It won't be negotiable. We can't risk a successful prosecution to satisfy anyone's art."

Val thought it over for a few seconds. "Fair enough, when will we hear from you?"

"I'll call you tomorrow." Leigh checked the time. "I need to go soon. Charity, we should probably set up your external access to files."

"Yeah, we gotta go get ready for filming." Val, blindly confident we would bend to her will, led Rory out.

It made me happy to see her lean into him as they walked, like teenagers in love. It was an intimacy she wouldn't have been capable of not that long ago.

I paid the bill. Val had left their drinks on our tab, but the waiter had comped them anyway. It pays to come to a local place.

We headed back to my home. Leigh had some encryption to run on my laptop that would allow me to access some non-critical files from home. I think she thought I was uncomfortable at the station. I wasn't, but I liked the idea of working from my place sometimes, away from official eyes.

I logged on and left her to work while I checked my cupboards for supplies. I always had great intentions of stocking my kitchen and cooking for myself, but I never did. Jake had been my source for all things domestic, but if Leigh was going to be working here, I should have some basics.

It occurred to me that Jake only popped into my mind twice in the last hour, and there was no reminder of the aching hole where our relationship used to sit. The past felt more like a fond memory than a raw wound. Perhaps I was making progress.

"Done," Leigh said. "Do you remember your password?"

I logged in to prove I knew how to. "Are you really going to get Rory permission to film?"

"I'll try, but he might not like the rules." Leigh checked her watch again. "I have to go, Charity."

"I thought we'd make decisions together," I said. If we didn't get this clear up front, I would barge over lines without knowing. Clarity wouldn't stop me from barging, but at least I'd know I was doing it.

"We should probably talk about that tomorrow," Leigh said. "No time to discuss it now."

She didn't give me a chance to say anything to delay her, just opened my door, said 'bye' and left.

So much for partnership.

Chapter 3

I'm not sure why I thought the cops would have a better system for grunt work than I'd come up with, but they didn't. Sitting in a cubicle making phone calls to check on the details in the file and trying to find a new lead didn't keep my attention focused. I was used to being on the road and doing stuff, not planning it. Some might say — okay, Matthieu, Lu, and Leigh all said — it's not a strength.

Having only half my focus on the work did give me the opportunity to watch the rest of the activity. A few people worked at desks, like me and Leigh, but most of the interesting stuff was happening in a glass-walled room in the corner.

I was too far away for a clear look. A whiteboard against the wall was covered in lots of lines and circles linking pictures and words. Similar to what you'd see on TV. Whoever was in charge had stuck some papers to the window, so I couldn't even pretend I could lip read.

The voicemail beep in my ear dragged me back to my task. "This is Charity Deacon. I'm working with the Vancouver Police and I have a few questions for you regarding what you witnessed on May 17. Please contact me when you receive this." I repeated my name and the number to call and then hung up. That was the third message in a row. If I was in charge, we'd make the calls when people were home, not in the middle of the day — who am I kidding? We would be knocking on doors and dropping in on workplaces.

Leigh was typing notes into the file; her boss was on the phone. Time to test if these guys wanted to share.

No one noticed when I stood and wandered toward the busy murder room. All the stuff on the walls might not be the murder case. It might be some organizational thing — I would be very disappointed if it turned out to be that.

I stopped to look at a workplace safety bulletin board and checked to see if anyone was coming to shoo me away. Still no one. And now I knew what to do in the event I got glass in my eye on the job. Not sure how it would happen in what is basically an office setting, but humans seem to always find a way.

I strolled toward the window. From this angle, the picture became clear. At the center of all the lines was Victoria LaSalle, the dead journalist. Not one of the crime scene pictures, although they were probably there somewhere. In this one, she must have been on location, a hot and dangerous place by the look of her bodyguard.

I assumed the lines led to suspects, but that could just be leads, since some of the faces were local celebrities. On the left of the board was a list.

Corruption - political, corporate, entertainment, police. The word police had been crossed out. I wondered how they could be so sure. Maybe it was denial.

Vice - nothing else listed.

Incompetence – again, nothing added. People would do horrible things to protect their reputation.

I figured I was looking at a list of the recent stories she was working on.

"Charity." Jill Kardozian, Leigh's boss. The tone didn't feel welcoming.

"Hi, Jill."

"Are you done with contacting witnesses?"

"Is that ever done?"

"Not if you spend your time watching other people work."

Apparently, existential questions were not on the agenda. "I needed to stretch my back." I gave her a big smile and headed back to the cubicle, unsure if it was procedure or if my history with the department put me under closer scrutiny.

"HOW ABOUT LUNCH?" Leigh's voice broke my concentration.

I checked the time. The best part of two hours had passed. I'd finished my phone calls quickly and spent most of the time since looking at the files.

I'd never had the opportunity in the past to work on three major cases. Mostly, I did the routine cases of any investigator: divorce, before it happened, when it was mostly catching a cheating spouse, or during the fighting when I needed to find hidden assets. I took a lot of insurance fraud cases and my surveillance skills were top notch. When something juicy came along, I focused on that exclusively.

Now, with all three files laid open, I made an effort to learn the police approach. When I compared the contents of the individual cases, I saw a lot of commonalities. Take statements. Compile crime scene evidence, when there is some. Document apparent connections. Follow up on those connections. From reading the files, it all seemed like a controlled process and using it would eventually lead to a few suspects and one of them would prove to be the culprit. Hindsight had a way of organizing chaos into something people could handle.

I needed to see the chaos in action. I know, it sounded like a handy excuse to get into that room.

"I could eat." I gathered my wallet and closed the files. Maybe over lunch Leigh would be more amenable to my suggestions.

Leigh led me out to the street. "I know a diner close by. We should be able to find a table at this time."

The walk was nicer than usual in this neighborhood. It wasn't exactly a bad area, but it was busy; narrow streets, trucks and cars, and lots of pedestrians. Today, the sun shone. There were only a few people around, and I didn't notice the traffic, probably because I was wondering why Leigh didn't just want to grab a sandwich and eat at our desks. Maybe I had a jaundiced view of how people work.

The diner was quaint in that *we were hipsters before it was cool* way.

Food ordered, coffee on the table, and no one hanging about, it was time to talk and I couldn't think how to raise the topic.

"What are your impressions so far, Charity?"

Leigh's words were casual, but I didn't become an investigator just because I'm nosy. My gut told me she was avoiding something, too.

"The cases are dead in the water, right?"

"I hoped not," she said.

The waiter put our plates in front of us. Me: fries and a BLT of sorts. Leigh: a big salad with some unidentifiable leaves and grains.

She dug out a few bits of avocado covered in tiny

sprinkles of bacon and chewed while she waited for me to answer.

I decided not to waste time. "What do you really want to ask?"

She poked at her salad again. I chomped on some fries while I deconstructed the sandwich to something I could actually get into my mouth for a bite. I didn't want to speak first, but she was good at putting me off.

Leigh put her fork on the table and glanced around. "It's not like I'm totally unfamiliar with investigations," she said. "I saw these were probably hopeless when I got them. I asked for your help because I thought you might have a different way of looking at them. Something that would give us hope of solving them."

She put a lot of faith in someone she kept telling to do things the official way. But maybe that was just under the gaze of her boss. In the diner, we were colleagues and couldn't get in trouble.

"Did you ever look at them together?" I asked. "I mean, as if they are one case?"

"You think they're connected?"

"No, or at least nothing in the files indicates they are."

"So, what's the point?"

Now I felt sympathy for Matthieu when he tried to install some professional processes to our work. My favorite question had been 'what's the point?' But his efforts had panned out and I made an effort to change my ways — not always, and not perfectly, but sometimes.

"For me, it was to look at what you, the cops, do when you investigate. Looking at each file as an exercise allowed me to see the common features. I found there are little gaps in all three, maybe nothing, but maybe new leads."

"You think someone left things out?"

Had I been accusing? "Not that I noticed. What I can't

tell is how the detective organizes the work as it goes along. See it live stream, if you like. The mess of the action can reveal clues," I said. It had happened to me a few times.

"We try to minimize the chaos," Leigh said. "Taking control of the case is important to collecting evidence that will hold up in court."

"That other case looks pretty chaotic," I said.

"They're gathering data that can be sorted and analyzed."

"How do they know when to stop?"

"That's something I need to learn. It's kind of an instinct according to a couple of detectives I asked. Lines of questioning are eventually completed, and you realize there is no new information. Then you start analyzing more and collecting less."

Instinct is only about fifty-fifty in my experience. "What about data from other districts?"

Leigh looked down at her salad. She'd managed to eat about half of it while we talked.

"We're supposed to have access, but other departments may not be up to date. And some of the information is unreliable because you can't talk to the detective who entered it. The other municipalities try to be helpful, but it means a phone call or two. The RCMP are Federal, so their systems don't line up well with ours."

She must have seen the look on my face, because she continued, "Not for the lack of effort, Charity. No one wants a criminal to go free because someone hoarded data. We are fighting a long history of different records and, yes, some different attitudes in the past. But there have been enough cases where the press found out we didn't share information to close a case faster, that we all try."

That hadn't been my reason for raising it, but it was good to know everyone was trying because we know how much trying accomplishes. "What about within your department? Other cases?"

She pushed her salad to the side and picked up her coffee. "You are not getting into the LaSalle case."

I thought I was being subtle. "If I could see how they work in the moment, it might help."

"We'll concentrate on the gaps you found." She signaled the waiter. "Charity, please don't screw this up for me."

She paid the bill and we walked back to the station. I looked toward the LaSalle case war room and caught the eye of the detective in charge. He glared at me and stepped over to close the door.

Chapter 4

Leigh seemed to think I was going to storm the gates of the LaSalle investigation. She sat beside me in my cubicle and made me show her the gaps I found. We used that to add a few more questions to our list and then planned out the appointments for the next day. Somehow the day slipped by and at four-thirty we were wrapping up.

"Please join me in my office," Leigh's boss said, creeping up again like a vampire.

I sat as Leigh stepped out of the cubicle.

"Both of you," she said, turning away and marching to her office.

"I promise I haven't done anything," I whispered to Leigh as I followed her.

"Shit," she whispered back. "Just let me do the talking."

We entered and stood to the side of the door. A man and a woman sat in two chairs across the desk from Sergeant Kardozian. The man wore a suit that had clearly been tailored to balance his slight belly, which would be invisible if he sucked it in. The woman sported a faux fur jacket — at least I assumed it was faux. Vancouver isn't cold enough to justify real fur to the activists, if it even could be done. The woman found a way to look down on us while she stared up.

"These are the people investigating my husband's murder?" She laced the words with a disdain I didn't know we'd earned.

"These two investigators are highly experienced," Kardozian said.

I kind of liked her attitude when it was turned on someone else. If I ever had to have a boss, Jill Kardozian wouldn't be the worst.

"Ms. Kardozian," the woman said, turning to look at her.

"Sergeant Kardozian."

"Of course." The woman flicked her hand in dismissal of such details. "I would love to hear how experienced. After all, my husband's case is languishing."

"Ms. Hargreaves, we assign the cases here. We don't let people choose."

So, Hargreaves was the wife of the poisoning case. They'd cleared her, Cecilie, if I remember correctly. I didn't think the investigation had gone deep enough; poison can be left to sit for a while or can accumulate to a fatal dose.

"Ms. Hargreaves, I assure you, we're going to find out who killed your husband," I said. "Could we meet with you? I have a few more questions about your trip that week."

"Are you accusing me?"

Kardozian stood. "I'm sure they are not. I'll leave you to talk, please use my office."

She walked out, and I couldn't help feeling she was happy to abandon us. I'd dealt with people like Hargreaves before. Poking her might get her mad enough to slip, or it might clam her up. By absenting herself, Kardozian was giving us a chance to provoke the woman and she could make all the apologies later. That, or she just didn't want to deal with her.

Even if I didn't think she was a viable suspect, Cecilie Hargreaves annoyed me enough I would happily treat her like one. Unfortunately, Leigh took over.

"The officer who interviewed you at the time did confirm your alibi," Leigh said. "I'm sure you understand there may be some details that are no longer as clear. It would be useful to check everything, so we can work on facts, not assumptions."

The man patted Hargreaves' knee. "Come on, C. If we don't help..."

I figured by the glare she sent his way that C didn't appreciate being handled.

"I didn't say I wouldn't help, Ernie, I just don't understand why the original officer isn't still working the case." She turned her attention to Leigh, fake tears in her eyes. "Isn't it important enough?"

"Every victim is important, Ms. Hargreaves," Leigh said. "After some time, we find that a new set of eyes can make a difference; a fresh viewpoint."

"Well, fine. Tell me how that worked in the past?" C asked.

Something about her voice was familiar. I hadn't seen her before...but the voice, I remember hearing it somewhere before.

"I'm an experienced officer," Leigh was saying, carefully keeping the details out. "I'm sure you and your husband will be satisfied when we close the case."

"And who are you?" C asked me.

It certainly felt like we were the subject of the interview. "Charity Deacon," I said. "If you have a few moments, perhaps we can get to our questions?"

"And your rank?"

She was not letting go.

"I'm a private consultant, ma'am."

"Not even police." C's voice struck a shrill note.

"I'm experienced in these kinds of cases," I said. "The department asked me to help out because Sergeant Kardozian wanted your husband's murder to be worked by the best."

Thankfully, Leigh didn't comment.

Cecilie Hargreaves stood and flicked her fingers at her husband. He jerked up and stepped toward the door. *Good little puppy.*

"Before you go, Mr.?"

"Ernie McBain." He held out his hand to shake; well trained in social graces. "Cecilie's second husband."

It felt weird that he thought we needed to know he was number two. Like he knew there would be a third.

"Mr. McBain, can we set up at time to meet? When can we ask these questions?" I wasn't letting them out before we had a date. And I suspected McBain had some information since their marriage happened so fast after the first Mr. C died. Nothing in the file, but I didn't trust a woman who didn't grieve.

"If you continue to harass us, I will have you removed from the case." Cecilie settled the fur around her shoulders and marched for the door.

"She's upset," Ernie said. "I'll smooth things over and set up an appointment."

They left before I could say anything more.

"Do you know who that is?" Leigh asked.

"I guess you don't mean just the victim's widow? Who?"

"Cecilie H Love. She had a pop hit about five years ago, *Roads of Love*, I think it was called."

That was where I'd heard the voice, some interview somewhere. "So that explains the diva attitude." No matter what happened to the case, I was going to get some answers from her.

Chapter 5

Leigh handled updating Kardozian and then we packed up. A quick drink at Cardero's turned into snacks and bitch session.

"You work within some rules, too," Leigh said as the waiter put her second glass of wine down on the bar.

I'd driven us to my place, then we walked over to the restaurant. She was taking a cab home and seemed determined to make it worthwhile.

"Nothing that can't be wiggled around if I need it. I don't break into homes — very often."

She laughed. "You only need to satisfy your client. We need to satisfy the Crown that we've got a solid case. They don't like having verdicts pulled from underneath them because we wiggled the rules."

I could understand, I guess. I knew where my lines were, what I would and wouldn't do for a case. And I've never been tempted to go over them, even a little.

But that's me. When you wield authority like the cops, you need group rules. You can't rely on the idea that everyone has the same lines they won't cross. That would easily get out of control.

"Fair enough. I only have to color in the lines while I'm working these cases anyway."

"Hey, you might find you like it." Leigh raised her glass like she was toasting the concept.

"Probably not, but Matthieu would be happy if I did. I haven't been able to soften him up as much as he's been making me more...professional."

"I'm not a little robot, Charity," Leigh said. "I just use my personal time for pushing limits."

I tried to imagine Leigh doing Roller Derby or riding a Harley. "Such as?" I asked when I couldn't form the image.

She ran her fingers through her hair. "I like rock climbing. I train for marathons. I can dance the tango." She laughed at the look on my face. "Did you think I went home and sat on the couch until bed?"

"I hadn't given it much thought, but I'm convinced. You're a wild woman living on the edge of danger."

"What about you?" Leigh asked. "I know Val and Lu are worried about you. I got enough pushing to try to make you social while Lu was gone. They think you're hiding from the world, but when you weren't healing from a breakup, what did you do?"

I hated questions like that. I liked my life, and yes, I was hiding a bit, but that was my business. The question just made me think the life I like, hanging out, going for lunch, walking around the seawall, watching movies, might not be as exciting or even as active as it should be. Judgment crept in, and not from other people. I felt like I had to justify my choices to myself.

"Nothing as exciting as you," I said. "I did travel for a few years when I was younger. Worked in Europe, explored a little of South America." There were some memories I kept hidden about that time. "I saw a lot of bad decisions, not all of them mine."

"So, you choose to float through life to avoid bad decisions?"

That cut a bit too close. I looked around for another subject. "Not exactly. Hey, check it out." I pointed to a street entertainer currently juggling a bowling pin, an apple and what looked like a hatchet. I didn't say I was subtle.

When I turned back to see if Leigh took the bait, a flash of something, sad and happy at the same time, crossed her face.

"Some bad decisions turn out to be the best thing that could happen."

I was going to ask her what she meant, but I sensed someone behind me. It was a bar, so people had come and gone around us all evening. We'd been careful about details as we talked because there was no privacy. But this felt a bit too close.

I turned. A guy was standing at the back of my stool rather than sitting at the empty one. He had a friend beside him. Both of them were looking at Leigh and me, ignoring the bartender who was asking for their order.

The one closest to me smiled. He did have a nice smile. And blue eyes and dark hair and he stood a few inches taller than me. His friend gave a chin nod aimed at Leigh. The friend was blond with hazel eyes, Nordic looking. Neither had an ounce of fat on their bodies — windsurfers or something.

"Nice evening," Blue Eyes said. "Are you hanging around?"

I glanced at Leigh. She checked her watch.

"I think we're heading out," I said.

"That is a pity," he said. "Can we convince you to stay for another drink? We have a table outside."

Was this how it was done these days?

"No. We're on our way as soon as we're done with these," I said, holding up my glass. There was too much for me to chug it — I know wine isn't supposed to be chugged — so I couldn't finish and walk out.

"Okay. Well, maybe we'll see you around," he said.

To give him credit, he said it with some regret. I watched them return to the table.

"Why did you do that?" Leigh sounded a little pissed.

"What? You need to leave by the look of it. You checked the time."

"I was checking how long I could stay. A drink with two nice guys wouldn't be the worst thing."

So, we probably needed to set up some signals. "Maybe they aren't nice."

"You and I are fully equipped to deal with any situation they could try to put us into." She sipped the last of her wine. "Next time, take a chance."

"I'm not ready for it," I said. I didn't say Blue Eyes reminded me of Jake. I wasn't ready for those memories.

"You won't ever be ready. You need to take a chance." Leigh pulled out her phone. "I might as well go."

"Hey, I'm sorry. What's the rush?"

"If we aren't going to sit with them, we should leave. It would be crappy for them to see us order another drink. There are some rules, Charity. You don't say you're leaving when you mean you're not interested. Just be honest."

"More rules."

"Yes, some rules make the game fun." She called the cab and walked away.

I looked at the two guys. Maybe he didn't look so much like Jake. Next time I would let Leigh do the talking.

. . .

WHEN I STROLLED into the bullpen the next morning, I was fully prepared for Leigh to still be annoyed with me. I had practiced an apology, and a suggestion of how to improve next time. Like a good little corporate girl. But she was fine with me and frustrated with the files. Good thing I'd been thinking about them all night.

"I think we're trying to do too much. We should concentrate on one case at first, move that along and then tackle another."

"We don't have forever, Charity. They're all important, and we need to solve them all."

"Yeah, I know. I'm not talking about spending weeks on one file. If we took today and tried to get traction on one case, then tomorrow we could look at the others. I think we're suffering from a lack of momentum."

She shrugged. "I can't think of a better idea and we have no interviews scheduled. Which one?"

I grabbed the Mary Copp file. "This is the one. She's still alive. She might wake up from the coma. We have a witness, and her case is the most current." There were other things I liked about it, but Leigh wouldn't approve.

"Did I miss something in the file?" Leigh flipped it open.

"Probably not, but I may be less confident in the information than you." I would come out and say I thought the cop who did the interviews was incompetent, but only if forced. That kind of statement needed to be defended and I was in the police station, after all.

"I've tried to get the witness on the phone," she said. "No luck."

"Yeah. Is that normal? People disappearing after

leaving a statement? Or should we be thinking he's a suspect?"

"Sadly, pretty normal. People move on with their lives. Even family members of victims usually give up hoping for justice eventually."

"Unlike Cecilie H," I said.

"Very much." Leigh wrote a few notes in her book, locked the file in a drawer, and stood. "Let's go to VGH. I don't remember anyone talking to the surgeon, or the nurses. Maybe Mary will suddenly wake up from her coma while we're there. Or maybe she's had some visitors we can contact."

Chapter 6

I thought the cops basically didn't run into the same problems I did when I tried to get information out of officials like this person at the front desk of the hospital. Mary Copp's bed was empty. Coma patients didn't walk around, so we assumed she was just being subjected to some tests. But no one on the ward was free to answer our questions. Here, in reception, no one seemed willing to answer them.

"It says she's having an MRI. I don't know how long the scan will take, or if they plan to take her back to her room afterward." The woman pointed to the screen facing her.

"Who is her doctor?" Leigh asked. "We can start our interviews there."

"Doctor Kareff is not in the hospital until tomorrow."

"Does someone check on her? Can I talk to the nurses?"

"You'll have to ask the ward nurses."

I didn't really understand why this woman was getting in the way. She should be helping us, giving us tidbits of gossip. I admit, Leigh's approach lacked a certain charm, but she was a cop.

I stepped up.

"We're trying to find out who put her here," I said. Now I was close enough to read her name tag. "Eileen, it was a nasty attack. We want to get him...or her off the streets. Don't you agree that would be a good idea?"

So, yeah, my brand of charm isn't subtle. Eileen hardened even more. There was something personal in her obstructiveness. Maybe she hated cops, maybe she thought we were going to blame the hospital for something, but this was definitely targeted at us.

"Of course, I want our streets safe," she said. "Harassing us isn't going to accomplish that."

I recognized a wall that wouldn't budge, so I tried another tactic. "We'll head up to the ward and wait," I said. "Before we go, does the record say who first examined Mary Copp when she came in?"

"Doctor Maynard." She read the words on her screen and stared at me, daring me to ask another question.

"Thanks." I turned and dragged Leigh away.

"She doesn't have the authority to do that," Leigh said.

"You're right, and you can call her supervisor, but I've had an idea." I drew her to the bank of elevators and pressed the down button.

"Mary is on the fifth floor."

"We'll head up later. The pathologist might be in."

"You think he'll talk to us?" She pulled out her notes. "Mark Karlsson."

"It might be worth asking. Maybe there's something he remembers that isn't in the report because it wasn't important at the time."

We exited the elevator onto a long, door-lined corridor. It was quiet and smelled of cleaning fluid and coffee. Like upstairs, there were painted lines to lead you around. We followed the morgue one, but Leigh seemed to know where to go without directions.

"No matter what happens," she said, "we're going back to the ward and talking to people."

I liked her determination.

The pathologist wasn't in, but his assistant was much more helpful than the receptionist. She pulled out the files and confirmed that we had complete copies. She answered a few questions that I had, but she didn't have all the information we wanted.

"His gut feelings don't go into the reports, but he'll remember, and he probably told the investigating officer at the time, but there are no notes to that effect."

She gave us an appointment in his schedule for tomorrow and suggested we meet him at a coffee shop rather than in the morgue. "Most people don't like being down here for long. I guess we get used to the smell."

Having someone be helpful had changed Leigh's mood. "Okay, let's hope the ward is quieter, Mary is back, and someone can talk to us," she said, stabbing at the elevator button.

On Mary's floor we walked into a different situation than before. The ward was calm and there were a few medical staff around who might have time to talk. I glanced into Mary's room, but she was still out for tests. I let Leigh lead the conversation this time, thinking the nursing staff might be a bit reluctant to discuss a patient with a civilian.

"She gets a visitor once in a while," Nurse Sue Ling said. "They don't check in, so we don't know who they are. Should we be worried about her? Do you think the person who attacked her will come here?"

"I don't think that's likely," Leigh said. "Too many

people watching all the time. She's safe here, probably more safe than at home."

"I can try to find out if her visitor would talk to you," Sue Ling said. "Would that work?"

"Thanks, that would be great," Leigh handed her a card. "What about her doctor, or the admitting doctor, how would you suggest we get in touch with them?"

Sue laughed. "Ah, you must have met Eileen. She takes her privacy duties a bit too far. I think if no one stopped her, even families would be banned."

"I thought it was just me," Leigh said.

"Let me check Mary's file." Sue went to a computer and looked up the record, then went to the paper version and made some notes.

She handed Leigh a sheet of paper. "Here's how you contact both doctors. You shouldn't have any problem getting on their schedule if you're flexible. I can't give you anything else, I'm skirting the edge of privacy rules as it is."

"Someone has to balance out Eileen," Leigh said. "Thanks, this might make all the difference."

Leigh headed for the elevator, but I walked past to the stairs.

"Where are you going?" Leigh asked.

"Don't you feel like a bit of exercise? Sitting at the desk all day?"

She shrugged and followed me. At the top of the stairs, I looked at the railing and the edges of the steps.

"Changed your mind?"

"I think this is where Victoria LaSalle fell," I said. I tried for a surprised, innocent tone but came up short.

"This is why you wanted to come here," Leigh said. "I can't interfere with that case, Charity. If you won't focus on our work, then I'll be forced to find another consultant.

Please don't make me start again. You had good ideas here."

I wondered if there was a connection between LaSalle's visit and Copp's being here. "Did they figure out why she was at the hospital?"

"How did you know the exact location?"

"I saw it on the news," I said. "And maybe I saw a picture on the wall of the war room."

"Unless you have a very good reason for looking at their evidence, you need to stop." Leigh's voice lost its kind of teasing tone. She was actually getting mad.

I didn't really have anything, not even the tiniest tingle. It just felt like their case would be more interesting than ours. "Okay, I promise. I'll control my curiosity. I will close my eyes if they drift in the direction of that room."

"Probably a good idea." Leigh turned and went back to summon the elevator. I followed, trying to demonstrate my ability to behave.

I couldn't quite stick on the good behavior list. "It's kind of odd LaSalle got killed here," I said as the elevator crawled down to the first floor.

"Most murders are crimes of opportunity," Leigh said in a tone that meant stop talking.

"But she goes into some pretty bad areas," I continued. If I kept talking, maybe she'd believe I couldn't read her subtle clues.

Leigh looked at me, her lips firming in what I hoped was reluctant agreement.

"Yes. If someone was planning to kill her, the hospital seems an odd choice. Someone might have found and saved her. Pushing her down the stairs isn't guaranteed to kill her, but it would incapacitate and make her easy to finish off."

"Do they know why she was here?" I couldn't get rid of

the idea that the opportunity came up because she was getting information from someone. That she was only killed to stop her spreading what she learned.

The elevator opened on the lobby. The usual number of visitors, ambulatory patients, and staff were wandering past. Everyone focused on their own worries.

"I'm not part of the briefing," Leigh said. This time there was definite resentment in her voice.

"I thought the daily briefings were for all cases."

"Usually, yes. But the LaSalle case is hot, and those briefings are closed. They don't want the press to learn any details that aren't officially released."

"They think you guys will leak information?"

"It has happened."

We crossed the overpass to the car park and after a quick search found our car. The lot was layered efficiently for packing the highest number of cars in the smallest footprint. The design meant if you took a wrong turn you could be wandering for a long time.

"Did she fall from the fifth floor?"

"As far as I know."

"Can we ask if they found out who she was visiting?"

"Why?" Leigh started the car. "No, don't tell me. You think she was here for Mary Copp?"

"It's possible," I said. It was worth a little hope if we got some information.

"Not probable, though. Copp wouldn't be able to talk to her. The nurse would probably have mentioned something if a journalist was asking questions."

I waited until we were parked at the station before I said more. When Leigh opened her door, I reached out to stop her leaving.

"Look, we need to talk," I said. "This is private enough."

She sighed but dropped back into her seat. "Okay."

"I know you don't want to wreck your career by stepping outside the rules. But I think you're doing damage by sticking too closely to them."

"I'm a cop, Charity. The rules are what keep us safe and get convictions."

"I'm not saying go rogue. But if you don't take any chances, you'll always be the one getting coffee and plodding through less important cases."

"The sergeant wouldn't do that to me," Leigh said without much conviction.

"She doesn't need to. You're doing it to yourself," I said. Why couldn't she see it? "Your boss is testing you, but not to find out if you're a good little girl. She wants you to prove you've got what it takes. Those guys on the LaSalle case, are they all Boy Scouts?"

"No." She turned to face me. "I have a lot depending on this promotion."

"What's the worst that could happen?"

"I get bounced back to uniform."

"You'd still have a job."

"One I hated."

"Even so, you would have one. If you take a few risks, and on balance you turn out to be right, then you'll keep this job, and you'll fit in," I said. I did understand the pressure she might be feeling, but Leigh was looking at this all wrong. "You used to be more flexible."

"I knew the boundaries of my old job," she said. "Now if I make a mistake, I'll be demoted or fired."

"Very unlikely." If I could just push her to try something, maybe she would understand what I meant. "Go to your boss and ask if you can look at the information. Tell her it may be linked to our file or it might not. Suggest it wouldn't hurt to close the line of inquiry or whatever you call it."

Leigh stared out the windshield. I hoped she was thinking about how she would approach Kardozian, rather than how she would finally shut me up. If she couldn't take a chance or two, we'd never solve the three cases. And I'd be ready to abandon her, which meant our friendship would never happen. As much as I resent the meddling, I did need more friends, and in spite of her current wishy-washy attitude, I liked Leigh. She was a badass. I just needed to nudge her into being that at work.

"Sounds reasonable." She opened her door. "I'm not going to break the rules, Charity, but maybe I can bend them a little."

All we got was a thank you from the boss. The upside was Leigh realizing she could push a little. For someone who rock climbed, she was really buttoned down at work.

Chapter 7

Today, we were meeting the pathologist at a Starbucks near the hospital. We hadn't yet managed to talk to the doctor who admitted Mary but held on to the hope Mary would wake up and tell us who chucked her over the seawall.

Our agreed strategy was that I would ask the questions, some we'd prepared and whatever I thought of as we went. Leigh would make notes and observe and then ask hers if I left anything out.

Mark Karlsson turned out to be a lookalike for Thor, if Thor was in his late forties. For someone who worked with the dead, he had a quirky sense of humor, or maybe that came from working with them.

"The two cases," I started as we sat around a tall table with our drinks and a couple of pastries. "Do you remember them?"

"I looked at them before I came, just in case I got them mixed up." He held up his phone. "The files are right here if I need them, and I brought my private notations. I think that is where the ghosts live."

I checked that Leigh was doing her thing. Her phone

lay on the table recording and she was scribbling notes on her pad. Mark said he didn't mind being recorded; he spent most of his life talking to a microphone since his patients didn't contribute to any conversation.

"Let's start with Jackson Tripton. Poisoned."

Mark gave a long nod and glanced at his phone. "Yes, Mr. Cecilie Hargreaves. Definitely murder. If he wanted to escape that woman with poison, there are many that would be easier to obtain and would hurt a lot less."

"Can you tell us a bit about the type of poison?" Our file had links to articles that had so many medical terms they seemed to be in a different language.

"Yes. Poisons are complicated sometimes. There are those which act reliably, strychnine or insulin for example, others not so much. They require a high dosage, or long periods of consumption to do their job. The victim often has time to seek medical help, and most are reversible if caught early enough. Then we have the isotopes, hard to get your hands on unless you're a spy or perhaps a terrorist. They are inevitable. We can only make the victim comfortable while they wait to die."

Interesting, if we were researching poison. "Tell us about aconite." When I looked it up online, all I found was some superficial information.

"The police brought the contents of Mr. Tripton's medicine cabinet. We noticed he used an 'herbal' supplement containing aconite in its safe form. Safe might not be the right word, but many people use the product to solve hair loss and other things. Now, that would not normally be a worry, but we routinely test these things. We found untreated aconite in the lotion, potent enough to kill quickly, and he was alone. His health was not good to start with and he wouldn't have had time to call for help."

"Any idea how the product, cream or a lotion, or a pill got contaminated?"

Leigh was watching closely now, pen poised above her notepad but unmoving.

"Possibly at the factory. They are unregulated, but this seems to be an isolated case. A cream, to answer your other question."

"What about the needle mark?" I asked. "I thought the poison was injected."

"No." He flipped through the file. "You may not have the final report. The needle mark was clean. I think whoever did it intended to misdirect the findings."

Interesting. "Any gut feelings?"

He sipped his latte before answering. "I leave the suspicions to the police and they cleared the wife. I assume he had enemies with access to the house." He paused. "But the wife would have the most access. I don't know if she had the knowledge. It's risky to get the dosage right. If she didn't know exactly how to handle it, we would have two victims to autopsy."

"Anything else seem odd?" I was losing hope we would get that one bit of a clue that solved the case.

"I mentioned Mr. Tripton's health was not great. I noted some indications that could have been interpreted as symptoms of chronic poisoning. Or they could simply have been the result of other 'herbal' remedies."

"What poisons?"

"Many, but probably cyanide. His medical records noted a recent history of headaches and shortness of breath that had no detectable cause."

I saw another search through internet medical resources in our future.

"Let's move on to Alex Sandhu. Stabbed."

"Yes, this was pretty cut and dried, if you excuse the

47

pun." He chuckled at his own joke. "The only thing I think I can add to the file is the person knew what they were doing. Five rapid stabs; the kidneys, the stomach and the chest; any of them eventually fatal, even with medical attention. But the killer disabled him first. It would have been fast."

"How much force would be needed?"

"With the right training and a sharp enough weapon, any average adult could accomplish it. Although I suppose the average adult does not get the right training or have access to the right weapon."

Leigh put her pen and pad aside. "Have you seen anything like this before?"

He chewed his lip in concentration. "No. I've seen stabbings, but by amateurs. Rage fueled. Sad to say, most of the men of Mr. Sandhu's age arrive on my table with gunshot wounds or as a result of an overdose." He held up a finger for us to wait and scrolled through the records on his phone.

I took the wait time to look up how one would get the training to kill by stabbing. It was scary how many hits I got.

"Yes," Mark said, interrupting my comment to Leigh. "As I said, most men in their mid-twenties come to me for very different reasons. I was struck by that, and I did mention it to the officer. Mr. Sandhu was not a saint by any means, but I found no drugs or alcohol in his system. He seemed quite fit, not a long-term marathon runner, but no couch potato. He was not someone I expected to cut up."

Mark had nothing more to offer but did say we could reach out to him if needed. I thought maybe that was directed more at Leigh than me; she had the official status, after all. Maybe my current lack of dating life was to blame, but I thought I recognized a little flirting going on.

As we walked back to the car, I mentioned to Leigh that I had been hoping for something more.

"You don't know if what we learned was the one thing we need in the case," she said. "We have a few more bits. And we have some direction to our research now."

I turned the corner into the bullpen. "Oh shit." I took a step back around the corner. Leigh passed me and walked right into the disaster.

"There you are!" Cecilie Hargreaves said as though we had an appointment.

I saw Leigh stop and, like a coward, I dodged back down the hall. It earned me a glare before she turned to face the drama queen.

"Were we expecting you?" Leigh asked, pretty politely I thought.

"You wanted to ask me questions," she said. "I am here to answer them. My friends convinced me I should help no matter how poorly you treat me."

The voices faded a little as Leigh must have been leading Ms. Hargreaves to a meeting room — that's what they called the interrogation rooms.

I figured the coast was clear when I couldn't quite make out the words. I stepped around the corner and saw the bullpen contained no divas or partners. I'd retreated too quickly to see if Cecilie was alone, but I expected her to have a lawyer or a husband with her.

The meeting room had an observation space beside it. I grabbed a notepad, slipped inside, and turned on the speaker.

"How did I feel?" Cecilie asked amazed. "How do you think I felt?"

Leigh sat across from Ms. Hargreaves, a small metal table between them. Today, no fur, faux or otherwise. Cecilie was dressed in a slinky red top with a chunky black necklace sitting just at the neckline, which hung a little too low for her age. Tight black jeans and matching boots completed the ensemble. Her giant studded purse sat beside her.

"I meant when you learned Mr. Tripton had been poisoned," Leigh said. "Of course, you were devastated when you heard of his death."

I liked the way Leigh didn't soften her words, like it was done to irritate the diva.

"I was shocked," Cecilie said. "I told him to stop using those off-the-shelf things. I told him bald could be beautiful. I wouldn't have worried about it affecting my image as a pop star. I mean look at Celine, her husband was so much older than she."

"Yes, your career," Leigh said. "Did his death get in the way of it? Were you too emotionally damaged to continue?"

"Of course," she answered. "But my fans demand so much of my life. They miss me. I get tweets daily asking when my next song will come out."

"Did you ever handle the 'off-the-shelf' things?"

"No! I had no idea what they would do to me. Some of them warned against allowing a woman to come in contact with the contents."

"Did your husband appear ill to you in the weeks prior to his death?"

Leigh's approach was getting to Cecilie. I figured she expected to come in, be treated kindly, cry a little, and then tell us we were taking too long. By the way she looked at Leigh, we wouldn't see her soon after this.

The best part was that every question was valid. Cecilie had nothing to argue with. And maybe our chat with Dr. Mark had fed Leigh some healthy suspicion. She was still my number one suspect, even with the alibi. I knew we'd have to prove it, but sometimes instinct showed the way. I just wasn't convinced Leigh agreed. After all, this could just be a tactic to keep a pest away.

Leigh stood. "Thank you, Ms. Hargreaves. I think we've asked all our questions. Do you have any travel plans?"

Cecilie stood and slung the purse over her shoulder. "Not yet, but my life tends to be hectic. You never know when I might be summoned to Nashville, or Hollywood."

In your dreams.

"Please let me know if you need to leave the jurisdiction," Leigh said, handing her another card. Then she turned and left Cecilie standing alone in the meeting room.

I stayed in the observation space until I was sure Hargreaves cleared the floor. Leigh was at her cubicle typing.

"That was interesting," I said.

"Coward," Leigh said.

"I owe you a drink." I sat on the edge of the cubicle desk. "Do you think she has something to do with it?"

"I wanted to get her off our backs at first. But she's cold and everything she said had the whiff of a lie. We'll see."

Chapter 8

Despite promising Leigh that I wouldn't get her in trouble by nosing into the LaSalle case, I couldn't help myself. No one had responded to our suggestion that LaSalle might have been visiting Mary Copp when she was pushed down the stairs. I didn't expect to be credited with solving the case, but a thank you didn't seem like too much to ask.

So, new tactic. I arrived at the door with a tray of Starbucks' coffee and treats.

"Hi, I know how things can drag in the afternoon when you need to be sharp, would these help?" Sweetness and light.

The head cop, Paul Grewal, grunted at me and pointed to the table. "Thanks, now what do you want?"

Man, that was harsh. I mean, yes it was a bribe, but couldn't he pretend that the coffee was simply kindness? "Did Sergeant Kardozian pass on our idea?"

"Yeah, I guess it could be a reason. Doesn't mean there is a connection between the visit and the murder." He picked up a chocolate croissant and stuffed half of it into his mouth.

"Is there anything I can do to find out if there is a connection?"

"You have enough to handle with the three cases she assigned," he said, a few crumbs flying out as he spoke.

"Yeah, the cases are tricky, but Leigh and I found some new leads," I said with the full knowledge that he'd been the detective on one of the files. "If we stumble on anything linking them, would you like us to tell you directly, or go through the boss?"

"Stay out of our way," he said. "Go through the boss. She'll figure out what's useful to us and what's just a hare-brained attempt to get information from me."

Well, that put me in my place. I was increasingly glad it wasn't my career on the line. "Fresh eyes can be useful," I said. "After all, we found some leads you missed, so I'm hopeful."

I didn't wait to be kicked out.

I turned to leave the room and bumped into another of the detectives. "Sorry," I said.

"Nice to meet you," he said back. "David Anchor."

I looked up at him, surprised at the lack of attitude in his words. Tall and red haired, he was smiling like we'd met at a church social. "Charity Deacon." I stepped around him before he could say anything more.

When I got back to my cube, I started to regret the final jab at Grewal's ego. This might not be my career, but it was Leigh's, and I would eventually need the cops to help me on some future cases. I'd just extended the deadline for being forgiven for outing one of theirs as a wife beater. Maybe I should send myself on a course about dealing with difficult people who you might need in the future.

We didn't make much progress for the rest of the afternoon. Now Leigh and I sat on my patio having some snacks and watching the boats go in and out. I was getting used to this after work wind down stuff. I would need to find a way to continue when I was back to working by myself.

"I get that you think we're bound by rules," Leigh said.

We were back on our philosophical discussion of how the cops worked at a disadvantage.

"I don't think it, you are." I pushed the bowl of chips toward her. Leigh was sipping a soda water and I had a glass of pinot gris. "Not only because you deal with evidence that has to stand up to a court case. It's everything."

She nodded toward the security gate. We could see over the roofs of the neighboring houses because it was low tide. At high tide, we floated up almost to street level. I liked the slightly different view as the day progressed.

I followed her gesture to see Val heading down the finger dock toward us. "Please take my side if she starts on the 'you need a guy' argument."

"I make no promises," Leigh said.

I heard the door close downstairs and a moment later Val appeared, soda in hand. "Don't you guys ever work?"

I laughed. "We're sharing opinions."

"On what?" She plunked onto the last chair.

"Leigh thinks the cops know the best way to close a case," I said.

"That's a little simplistic," Leigh said. "We have different ways, and when in Rome..."

Val pouted in thought. "So, if you were working on a case for Charity, like you were on vacation and needed something to do, you'd work by her rules?"

"Yeah, when in Rome..." I said.

"First of all, when I'm on vacation, I never need something to do. Secondly, on a civil case, yes. I can be flexible."

I hadn't thought about it in reverse. "You'd be

surprised how hard it is to do that," I said. "It's not like I don't try to do as the Romans do, I just think you do things the hard way."

"Yeah," Val said. "Like this work I'm doing for Rance. I gotta follow all these guidelines, that's what they call rules. If they really were guidelines, no one would freak out when I did things right instead of by the rules."

Leigh and I both laughed at that.

"See, you're both the same," Leigh said. "You think yours is the only right way to do things."

"Okay, maybe I used the wrong word," Val said, dipping her hand into the bowl of chips. "But I could do the job in half the time if they let me organize it."

"It's not all about speed," Leigh said.

"It is for me," I said. "The faster I can close a case, the more clients I can take in."

"That sounds like you don't care about the end result," Leigh said.

"Yeah," Val said. "Like my job, there's more than one right way and faster should be better. But I have it easy. I have files to image and then I'm done. You guys have to find out who the bad guy is, or how they did it, or if they did it." She shrugged. "Charity's stuff is more complicated, I guess. What I mean is you don't get to check things off a list and then move on."

"Charity's cases are more varied," Leigh said. "Ours are more complicated."

The conversation was getting a bit too serious for me. "Not a competition," I said. "Name one thing I need to change."

"There are so many," Leigh said, laughing. "Okay. The biggest thing in our way is that you don't under-stand how to work within the politics. You keep causing issues without even thinking. Then I spend time smoothing things out when I should be working on the case."

"Matthieu said he was surprised at how good I was at teamwork."

"Different thing," Val said.

"How do you know?" Val and I had worked as a team, when she was willing, but she'd always been a lone operator otherwise.

"Rance." She shrugged. "He kind of coaches me. I think he's expecting me to take a permanent job with his firm. But he says all organizations have a political culture." She used air quotes. "Work is not so much about getting things done; you also need to keep the road clear."

"Good analogy," Leigh said.

I liked how I heard Rance's influence in the way Val talked, but I was starting to feel ganged up on again. "Like how?"

Leigh finished her soda. "Every time you antagonize the LaSalle team, I need to calm them down."

"But if everyone shared, we would probably solve the cases faster."

Leigh stood. "That's the usual philosophy, but you forget that the LaSalle investigation is all over the media. They are under a lot of pressure not to screw up. Having a new detective and someone they see as an amateur horn in, is risking bad press. Bad press gets in the way of the investigation."

I felt my cheeks burn. "I didn't think of it like that."

"I know, but now is a good time to start. I have to go."

Chapter 9

Don't antagonize; be smooth.

When Val left last night, I couldn't stop mulling over what she'd said. Advice from Leigh I expected, even if I didn't agree, but when Val chimed in, I couldn't ignore it. So, here I was at seven a.m., not a time I was used to seeing, in the office to take a quiet look at the LaSalle file when no one was around so I wouldn't cause problems. Maybe that wasn't the purpose of the advice, but I accept that I'm not perfect.

The lights came on as I walked toward the war room. Automatic, nothing to worry about. The lock wasn't a high security one. A quick poke with my picks would open it, and no one would know I'd been inside.

Yes, I felt guilty, who wouldn't? If everything went to plan, great. One thing goes wrong and I'm off the case, Leigh's in deep shit, and maybe the case gets blown. That's true, but not very likely.

As I passed my desk, I noticed the blinking light on the phone. Someone finally returning one of my calls? I stopped. The message would still be there when I finished in the war room. But no one would be around for a half hour at least if the past few days were the norm.

When I took a step, my curiosity battled with my sense of responsibility — not a fight I was used to. Leigh's voice in my head said check the message. My own little conscience said do something right before you screw everything up.

I picked up the phone just to check what was on the message. I could always listen closer later.

"Hi, I got your message. Sorry it took so long. I was out of town for a few days. I'm happy that someone is looking at Mary's attack again. I'm her sister, Lila May, in case I forgot to mention it. Of course, I'll take some time to speak with you." The woman left her phone number and ended the call with another apology for being away.

At last, a break to work on.

I wrote a note for Leigh and dropped it on her desk. There was a form sitting on the keyboard. I glanced at it. An authorization for Rory to film us. Crap. Maybe I could make a deal with him to not film me when I was doing something like I was about to do.

I tucked my lock picks into my hand, palming them to keep the possibility of secrecy in case someone walked in at the wrong moment.

I wandered to the war room door. I tested the handle — locked. I looked around, took a deep breath, and let my picks slide into my fingers. Reached for the handle again.

Heard voices in the hall.

Froze for a second.

Glanced at the papers pinned to the wall while I palmed the picks again.

Turned to walk away.

Smiled at Leigh and Rory as they rounded the corner.

Shit!

At least I wasn't actually inside the room. I tried to pretend nothing was happening by launching into the message from Mary's sister. "So, we should probably go ahead and set up an interview, right?"

Leigh either bought my act or decided to play along. If it was the second, then I was a little closer to getting her on my side.

"Rory, the agreement is on my desk," she said, pointing to the paper. "Read it before you sign. The conditions are not negotiable."

"My dad would freak if I signed something without reading," he said, sliding into the cube. "Do I get a badge like Charity?"

"Not the same, and not free access."

Leigh pulled me aside. "I thought we agreed to leave that case alone," she said.

"We didn't exactly," I said. Then, seeing the look in her eyes and wanting to stay on our assignment, I added, "Yeah, I let you think that. Leigh, my gut says there's something there. I can't put my finger on it without taking a look at what they have."

"If you're right, and I'm not saying you are, something in our cases will give us the key. How would you feel if they came poking around our stuff just on a hunch?"

She knew me too well to believe I'd be happy with that. "They already had all ours," I said. "Tell me, are they likely looking for connections? With our cases, I mean?"

Leigh glanced over to the empty room. "Maybe, but the LaSalle case is more complicated. She didn't play politics, so she has a lot of enemies. It doesn't mean they all wanted her dead, but the odds are it's one of the people she wrote about. Our victims? I think they'll end up being more run of the mill, spouse, rival, clear connections we haven't figured out yet."

"If we find something," I said, "something else that connects them, will you push for access then?"

Leigh sighed. "I'm not fighting you. I do trust that you have instinct, Charity. Of course, I'll push for information from the LaSalle team."

"Okay, we should go find something."

"The sister seems like a good place to start," Leigh said.

"We'll get a break on the others too," I said. "Maybe we'll be really lucky, and it will turn out to be the spouse in the Tripton case."

"I'd be happy if the next break led to closing that one and getting her off our backs. Imagine how much worse it is for Paul on the actual hot case."

He deserved it, we didn't. I was smart enough to keep that thought to myself.

"All signed," Rory called to us. "When are we going to start kicking butt?"

"The optimism of youth," Leigh said.

"Rory won't be a problem," I said. "You know Val is pulling the strings. She's got a plan for their future, so she won't let him do anything to lose access to these cases."

Chapter 10

"I'll call Lila May back and we'll find out what she has for us," Leigh said, waving Rory out of her way.

Rory lifted the camera to his shoulder.

"Are you going to start filming now?" she asked. "Me making a call?"

I stepped back. This was something for Leigh to work out.

"Yeah. Is there a problem?"

She pursed her lips and then shrugged. "I guess not. You'll need permission from people we interview before filming."

"Yeah, I read the papers." He reached up and pressed a button on the side of the camera. "Just do your thing and forget I'm here."

Leigh dialed the number Lila May had left us. There was a pause and she said, "Ms. May, this is Detective Andrews returning your call. We would like to set up a time to meet. Please call my personal phone." She rattled off her contact information and hung up.

"We could go over to her place," I said.

"We'll do that if she stops being willing. I don't want to antagonize her into withdrawing her help." Leigh pushed a few papers around. "Too bad, that was about our only lead."

I was tired of waiting for people to give us information. "Not really," I said. "We have a bunch of people who aren't responding to us. How about we see if they can be antagonized into helpfulness."

A smile flickered on and off. "How? I mean, how without getting a bunch more complaints like the cranky widow?"

"Jackson Tripton. His case, I mean. If his widow is so willing to jump all over us, maybe we shouldn't be so patient."

"It's likely to bring her down heavier on us," Leigh said.

Rory moved to put his camera on both of us. I tried to ignore him.

"At least we'll catch hell because of something we did, not just her bitching about us not doing something."

"I'm not going to jump on people at random to find out if we spark a reaction. It doesn't work in real police investigations, Charity. We need a reason."

"My gut is telling me we'll find one. And think about how much easier it will be to solve the other two cases if we get her off our backs."

"I kind of agree with Leigh," Rory said. "Having people freak out when you accuse them of all kinds of things is good for ratings, but I want to show how investigations really work. My dad said he's tired of juries thinking everything is like on TV and getting frustrated when there's no DNA, or other stuff, overnight."

Why was it a surprise that Rory sided with Leigh? He might look like a rebel, but he was Rance MacDonald's son. He'd be shy of bumping up against the fences, let alone jumping them.

"I think it's too early in the investigation to worry too much about what a jury will think," I said. "Leigh, you can't be happy that we've spent all this time only poking through files and leaving messages."

"No kidding. Okay, where do you want to start?"

"Relatives?" Tripton didn't have many, but we had one or two on the list, and he had a past in Calgary.

I pulled the list of contacts from the Tripton file.

"Detective Andrews, Ms. Deacon, I want an update." Leigh's boss stood behind Rory. "You can wait outside, young man. This doesn't need to be recorded."

That sounded ominous. She didn't say we had to keep Rory out of it after the meeting. I gave him a nod that I hoped was reassuring. If he couldn't record everything, it might be a boring documentary no matter how much editing he did. Apparently, he had more political savvy than I did because he turned off the camera and sat in Leigh's cubicle.

We followed Sergeant Kardozian into her office. I closed the door behind me and took the seat she offered. It didn't feel like we were about to be reprimanded, but it also didn't feel like we weren't. I'd have to figure out how she did that; it would come in handy when I talked to suspects.

"Update me on the three cases," Kardozian said, sitting back in her chair.

I let Leigh do the talking, pretty sure I would make things worse.

"We talked to the pathologist about the Tripton and Sandhu cases. We will be contacting the admitting physician for the Mary Copp case."

"New information?"

"Mary Copp's sister contacted us."

"I meant on the Tripton case."

"The pathologist provided some insights the official report didn't include. How the poison could have gotten into his system, for instance."

"Why wasn't this in the file?"

Cecilie was clearly putting pressure on the sergeant, too. I had the urge to ask if we should forget about the other two cases because no one was asking questions, but even I knew that was not a good path to step on.

"I can't be sure without talking to the original detective," Leigh said.

"Detective Grewal has his hands full and I want him focused. What is your guess?"

Leigh nodded. She was stalling for time, I knew. Trying to figure out how to not sound like a bitch.

I liked my life much better right now. Politics just wasted time and you couldn't ever make them go away.

"If it was me, I might not have recorded the pathologist's guesses in the file unless they came to something. Maybe Paul took some notes he kept outside the official file?"

"I'll ask him," Kardozian said. "What else?"

"We've left messages to re-interview people, but no one responded. We were planning to do some drop-bys today."

"I know cold cases are hard, Leigh. Normally I would have you paired with a more experienced detective. But circumstances don't allow it. Between you and Deacon, you have the skills. I expect you to do what it takes to get a conviction."

"Thanks, Sergeant." Leigh didn't look at me.

"I want to be able to answer Cecilie Hargreaves' questions when she calls. You need to keep me in the loop, so I can do my job."

"What exactly does that mean?" I asked.

"Keep me updated on your actions; daily will work unless you think you're going to cause some problems. I'm not saying soften your approach, I'm saying give me a heads up."

"And what's your job?" I asked. I could tell Leigh wanted to shut me up, but I needed to be really sure what Kardozian expected. Not that I was planning to let her control us, but it would be nice to know when we were about to land in trouble. "I mean, I don't understand the hierarchy here. Just want to be clear."

Kardozian tapped her finger on the desk. "Primarily, in the Tripton case, I need to be able to deflect attention, like in the LaSalle case. Having too much scrutiny on an active investigation isn't productive. I talk to Hargreaves, I talk to the press or bring a media expert in. Your job is to find the killers."

Not the reaction I expected. I wondered how much of Jill Kardozian's stern boss act was an act.

"Okay," I said.

"Send me a list of who you're seeing today," Kardozian said. "I won't share it with Hargreaves, but I need to be up to date."

Leigh stood and opened the door for me. I couldn't tell by the look on her face if she was angry, thankful, or relieved.

Chapter 11

Back at her desk, Leigh lifted the three files. "We are not just going to concentrate on Tripton," she said. "Just because his widow is making noise doesn't mean the other two cases aren't important."

"But?" I said. "But it will keep everyone happy if we do, right?"

"Not me, and not Mary Copp's sister, or Alex Sandhu's family." She turned to Rory, who was standing with his camera aimed at Leigh's face. "We solve cases, not public relations problems."

"Okay. So, when Lila May calls back, we go to her?" I asked.

"If she doesn't call back today, we'll drop by. Until then, we look at the two actual murders."

I liked this new Leigh. Maybe her boss knew something about managing detectives.

"How about we drop in on Ms. Hargreaves? She should be easy to find."

"We'll put her aside until there's a reason other than to piss her off," Leigh said. "Let's talk to Tripton's best friend.

You try the admitting physician for Mary Copp. I'll send the list to Kardozian after we leave."

"List?"

"We'll start with Harvey Richards, and if he gives us any information that leads us on, I'll text her."

"Is that what she wanted?" Rory asked. "I should have been in there. Even if someone vetoes using what I film, I should record."

Leigh nodded for me to answer as she picked up the phone. I drew Rory over to my cube.

"The sergeant wanted to be kept in the loop so she could handle Cecilie Hargreaves," I said. "Leigh probably knows more about how to do that than me. I agree you should have been there, but you didn't miss anything."

"Should I go talk to the sergeant? Do you think she didn't want me around?"

At least someone thought I was good for advice on this stuff. "I think that's a good idea, Rory. You don't want Leigh to do it for you, but tell her and ask her how you should do it."

"Don't screw with her reputation?" Rory laughed.

"Exactly."

Leigh stood and grabbed her jacket. "Let's go. Richards is waiting for us in his office."

HARVEY RICHARDS SAT behind the desk in his office at Richards and Associates Talent Agency. I didn't know about any associates, but we'd been greeted by a receptionist who looked like she might have been someone semi-famous in her youth. She'd led us past an open area holding ten workstations with someone on the phone in each. Like a mini call center, there was only a soft murmur of voices. The only other office I'd seen was empty of anything but a desk, a chair, and a phone.

We didn't plan in advance how to conduct the interview, so I played sidekick.

Leigh was doing the introductions. Harvey smiled, rubbed his bald head, and held out a cigar-stained hand for shaking. If he received a casting request for a typical talent agent, he could assign it to himself. Probably fifty, overweight, and artificially tanned, he made me feel like I should be checking my wallet to make sure he hadn't taken his ten percent.

When he started talking, the image disappeared. His voice was soft, and I swear he'd been crying before we came.

"I should have called you back sooner," he said. "I know how important it is for the police to get all the details early. I just...I've been having difficulty dealing with the loss. Jackson and I have been...were friends for years. Jackson was the one who inspired me to come to Vancouver. I would still be in Calgary representing catalog models if not for him."

I jumped into the pause he took to breathe. "You gave a report at the time," I said, trying to reassure him. It was great to have someone so willing to talk. We just needed to keep him on track. "We're here to follow up on that."

"And if you remember anything new," Leigh added. "Sometimes as the shock fades, more details come up."

He wiped at his head again. "Yes. Well as it happens, Jackson was the business head here. I'm not sure how long I can go without someone to replace him. Maryellen has helped, but..."

"Maryellen?" Was that a new lead?

"My receptionist. You met her." He sat up straighter. "Did she offer you coffee?"

"Yes, but we're fine," Leigh said.

"And the young man?" Harvey pointed to Rory. "If you are looking for an agent, I highly recommend our agency."

"Thanks, I'll think about it." Rory moved closer. "I just need to get some establishing shots."

"You can't film my clients," Harvey said. "That includes the people working here. They are all clients."

Rory nodded and continued aiming and focusing his camera.

"You were saying that Mr. Tripton was the business head?" Leigh took out her notebook.

"Yes. In the process of dealing with the records, I found some old photos. They brought up memories. I don't know why I didn't think of it before."

"Memories?" My turn to prompt. It was difficult to watch his grief, especially since the dead man's wife had moved on so quickly.

"Oh, yes." He pulled a paper from a drawer. "This is a list of clients that Jackson brought to the firm, and ones he tended to handle himself. Perhaps one of them will give you some insight."

Leigh took the list and snapped a photo. "This might be very helpful."

Harvey smiled at that, then he clasped his hands and rested his elbows on the desk top, like he was about to launch into a heartfelt prayer.

"There is one more thing," he said. "I have no idea if it will be of use. I don't know the details and tried not to speculate. But...well, before we came here, before Jackson and I formed the firm, he was engaged to a lovely girl. But it suddenly came to an end. Within a short time, too short really, he was engaged and then married to Cecilie Harg-reaves. That one hit wonder? I'm sure you've met her."

"Did Tripton call off the wedding?" I asked.

"He wouldn't talk about it and I respected his privacy. But...I have a name for you. Althea O'Brien. She's still in Calgary as far as I know. Maybe she can tell you."

We spent a few more minutes listening to Harvey's business woes. He didn't seem to see the solution was in Maryellen, who he credited with every move but didn't consider partner material.

"We'll let you get back to it," Leigh said as she stood. "Thank you, this may all lead to the killer."

"Do you have a suspect?" Harvey asked.

"We can't comment on an ongoing investigation," she said.

"So Cecilie is still cleared," he said, sounding disappointed.

As we headed for the car, Leigh's phone rang. She beeped the lock and I got in the front, Rory in the back.

Leigh ended her conversation and joined us. "Lila May can see us now. At Mary's house." She pulled away without giving any more information.

Chapter 12

Mary's house was on a small lot in East Vancouver, near the Nanaimo Skytrain station. Pretty typical, cracks in the stucco, fenced back yard, small front yard, two floors and a basement. As we approached the bright blue door, it opened and someone who looked very much like Mary Copp, tall, lean, pale with dyed red hair, stood aside to let us in after checking Leigh's ID.

"Lila? Did Mary rent?" I asked. If she was about to be evicted, we needed to do a thorough search today.

"No, she bought this place with her share of our mother's estate. I'll make sure the utilities and taxes are paid while she's gone."

That was a little pressure off.

"Can I confirm we have your permission to look around?" Leigh asked. I guess so Rory could get it on record.

"Yes. Other police officers came before but found nothing," Lila said.

"I'm sure you've answered these questions before,"

Leigh said. "If you don't mind, sometimes a fresh look uncovers something."

"Oh, ask away. Mary had her problems, but no one deserves what happened to her. I pray every day she will wake up, but my heart holds no real hope."

That was probably the saddest thing I'd heard in my life. "What kind of problems?"

Lila escorted us through the main floor, a front room, small and crowded with furniture, a bathroom, and an eat-in kitchen. "She sometimes lost perspective. When we were kids, she would get absorbed by an interest and nothing could intervene until she decided to move on."

"Lots of kids do that," Leigh said. "Dinosaurs, Poké-mon. What was different for Mary?"

"That is hard to explain," Lila said. She pointed to the stairs. "There are two bedrooms and another bathroom. I'll let you go up by yourselves."

Leigh waited for her answer. "Can you try to explain?"

"Oh, yes. Sorry, I...well, it wasn't so much that she got excited about things. As you said, we've all got our passions. For Mary though...she focused on people or obscure knowledge. If all the genealogical research stuff was around when we were kids, our family tree would be mapped out to Adam and Eve."

Lila offered us coffee or tea, but we declined. I don't know if it's a cop thing, not taking refreshments from witnesses, but for me, I just thought about how long Mary had been in the hospital and figured anything in the kitchen would be undrinkable.

Two rooms upstairs yielded nothing. Both used as bedrooms, but one obviously a little used guest room; just a bed and one night table occupied the floor space. The bathroom was tiny, probably started life as a third bedroom and lost space in a renovation, no hidden panels, no pills or liquor hidden in the towel rack.

"This was a waste of time," Rory said. "Shouldn't we be following up on the other case?"

Leigh gave him a look that stopped his next statement. "We aren't done yet. Investigations are about tiny details. We already found one piece of information that wasn't in the file. And you aren't part of the investigation other than recording, Rory. Are we clear?"

I felt bad for him. If Leigh spoke to me like that I might blow up, or crawl away. Rory nodded. "Clear."

"He's got a point," she said. "It's not really enough."

"We can always come back if we need to," I said. "Maybe Lila will give us a key?"

"We'll finish what we came for. There's the basement, and I'd like to check out the yard. We don't take keys from people, but we do need access. I'll see what we can do."

Downstairs, Lila was pouring boiling water over a teabag. "Anything?"

"I can't say," Leigh said. "Did you want to come to the basement with us?"

Lila shook her head. "It feels like I'm snooping. Mary wouldn't like it."

I guess she'd be okay with us snooping because we have a reason.

In the basement we found the concrete floor swept clean. Two posts held up the floor above. No boxes, no patio furniture, nothing.

We backed up and checked the yard. Nothing.

I hoped Leigh was right about the tiny details making a difference because that's all we had.

"We may need to come back." I heard Leigh say to Lila. "Can we call you to let us in?"

"That might be inconvenient for you," Lila said. "I'm not always available."

"Can we arrange to put a lock-box in? We could do that today." Leigh pulled out her phone.

"That would be acceptable to me," Lila said. She sighed. "Mary will probably throw a fit. But if she wakes up, then I'll happily take the flak."

Leigh made the arrangements and we left.

Chapter 13

When I got in the next morning, Leigh was waiting. "I want to drop in on the Sandhus. See if our luck holds and we learn something about him."

It felt great to actually be doing something other than reading files. I turned to go back to the car park.

"This is the dude who was stabbed?" Rory asked. "You think maybe someone he knew did it?"

"I don't make assumptions," she said as the elevator arrived. "What makes you ask that?"

Rory shrugged and played with his camera.

When we left the parking lot, Leigh turned east onto 2nd so we could jump on the highway. The traffic was getting heavy with mid-morning rush hour. It was going to take a while to drive out to Surrey, where the Sandhu family lived. Normally the RCMP would investigate, but Alex had been stabbed in Pacific Spirit Park, so the case remained in Leigh's jurisdiction.

"Who are we meeting?" I asked. I'd left messages for Alex's family, mother, father and a couple of siblings, but no one had called back.

"We're seeing who's in," Leigh said. "Your idea of dropping in was a good one. If the Sandhus aren't home, then maybe a neighbor will be."

I'd had good luck in the past chatting with neighbors. No matter how much you think you keep to yourself, there's always someone who knows your business.

"When I asked that question," Rory said from the back seat, "I didn't mean because he was probably a gang member."

"What did you mean?" I asked.

"Isn't it usually someone close to you?" He looked out the window. "I've been researching murder. For the documentary. Stabbing is usually one of two things. A fight that goes wrong, or someone who loves you."

Leigh pulled on to the highway. "Yes, usually. But we can't just assume things are the usual. We have to look at each case separately. If we don't, we'll miss something."

"I get it." Rory leaned forward between the seats. "If I read the files, I could help. Maybe I can give you some ideas. You know, as someone with a fresh look?"

I suddenly had an inkling of how annoying I might be about the hot case. I needn't have worried about Rory. He was going to push against the rules as much as possible. I tried to justify my actions as important to the case. I'm guessing Rory thought his suggestion was something similar to my justification.

"You can't use anything in the file." Leigh swung around a semi. "I can't let anything taint the case."

"I wouldn't film. I wouldn't tell anyone what I saw."

"It's over my pay grade."

Did Leigh know that she just told him to go over her head?

"So, how do I get a meeting with your boss?"

Leigh glanced at me, like it was my fault.

"I mean, she doesn't seem to want me around. I thought I should talk to her and assure her that I wasn't going to be a problem."

Leigh groaned. "I'm going to regret getting you permission to film, aren't I?"

"No," Rory said, too quickly to sound reassuring. "I promise you'll be glad I'm here."

"Let me think about it." She sped up as we approached the exit. "I'll do the talking unless I tell you to jump in." She glared at me.

I put on my innocent face. "Absolutely."

When we pulled up outside the Sandhu house, we saw movement inside. No cars in the driveway, but the garage was closed. Pop music leaked through an open window.

Leigh knocked on the door. When no one answered, she rang the doorbell. Still no reaction.

"Definitely someone home," I said. "Let me go look through the window."

I didn't wait for an answer. Rory followed me and we crossed the lawn to the side of the house. The window was too high to see through, but I heard someone singing along. Not very well, but enthusiastically.

"Hey!" I yelled as loud as I could.

The music went quiet and a young girl answered, staying out of sight. "Who are you?"

Before I could answer, Leigh knocked again and called out "Police!".

"Shit." I heard someone scrabbling to tidy up — or hide the dope I smelled.

Rory and I headed back to the front door just in time to see it open. A girl in her late teens stood there, trying to seem sober — I knew that expression from my own youth. She could have been a model, but she wore a tee shirt and sweatpants, no makeup, her hair in a braid.

"Come on in, officer."

Leigh introduced us and asked if she was okay with Rory filming.

"Sure, but give me a minute." She ran upstairs.

"I'm guessing that was the sister," I said. "Parm?"

"Yeah. And I think we need to tell her we don't care about a little dope smoking. At least it isn't an opiate."

We stood in the living room looking around and waiting for Parm to return. I tried to see the house as a place of grief, but there was no indication that they'd lost a son. Pictures on the mantle and wall showed Parm through the years and a younger boy. A few of Alex, and a bunch of other relatives.

"Okay, we can film now," Parm said.

She came down the stairs a different girl. Still young looking, but now wearing a bright blue sari, jewelry, and more makeup than I could have put on in the short time she'd been gone. She was dazzlingly beautiful. No amount of clothing or cosmetics would transform me that much.

"Are your parents around?" Leigh asked.

"They went to India a month ago with my brother. The other one. Said they needed to go away for a while."

Leigh looked around. "And you are alone until they come back?"

"Auntie looks in every day, but I'm eighteen. They trust me." She bit her lip. "You won't tell them about..." She waved her hand as though the room was filled with smoke.

"We don't care about that," Leigh assured her. "I'm working on your brother's case. I hoped to get some more information from your parents."

"Like what?"

Rory moved around the room, getting some shots of the whole setting. Parm watched him carefully, making sure he didn't catch her frowning, I guess.

"We don't have a lot about your brother as a person. If we know more about him, it might help us find whoever stabbed him."

"Like on TV?" Parm asked. "If you can figure out why someone wanted to kill him, you can find them?"

"Sort of." Leigh pulled out her notebook. "What kind of person was Alex?"

Parm didn't show the slightest sadness talking about her older brother. I liked her less as the interview passed.

"He was like an okay guy. He worked out. He had a job. He met the women that mom found him to marry. He didn't have any girlfriends. I thought maybe he was gay. But that wouldn't go over with the parents. He bought me nice things sometimes."

Leigh made a few notes. "Did he like his work?"

"Yeah, I guess. I mean it was his business, so he must have loved it."

"Do you know who his clients were?" Leigh asked.

"No. Like people who needed PR, like celebrities and stuff."

"What happened to his files?"

"Dad got them from his apartment. Alex's stuff is in the basement. Do you want to look in them?"

She might not be the most emotional sister, but she was willing to be helpful.

"Yes, and if it's okay, we'd like to take them with us." Leigh checked her notebook again. "Any idea why he ran down by UBC? There are some trails here, in Surrey."

"He was training for something. I forget what. But the park was the closest to the actual race conditions that he could find here. Um...are we almost done?"

"Do you know what gym he worked out at?"

"Yeah, the one in the Richmond Oval. Oh, I never thought about that. He didn't really train around here. He lived not that far away, but I guess he liked other places better."

Leigh stood. "Let's see the files and then we can leave you to your day."

Parm led us into the basement. The boxes were in the living room of an in-law suite. There were four, all labeled Alex. Leigh wrote a receipt and asked if Rory would help load them in the car.

"Parm, this is an open investigation," Leigh said. "It would be better if you didn't gossip about this with your friends. Or post online."

"Oh. Okay." She looked at Rory, who'd turned off his camera and picked up one of the boxes. "Will I get to see what he filmed? Will I be able to say if he can use it?"

"Yes," Leigh said without checking with Rory. "He won't put anything out there without permission. I'll make sure you see it first."

Rory came back and put his camera on top of a second box. Leigh and I hefted one each and we filled the car. Parm stood watching as we drove away.

Chapter 14

We stopped for lunch on our way back. Rory was hungry...well, so was I, but he complained the most.

We sat in a White Spot and waited for our food. The place was busy, but that meant no one but the wait staff paid attention to us. Rory's camera sat beside me on the bench. Apparently, the restaurant was a little camera shy and the manager said he couldn't film.

"So, what do we have?" I asked. "New, I mean."

"Hey, I haven't seen the files, remember," Rory said. "Maybe you should tell me what you know in total? Maybe hearing the whole story will help the investigation." He put his phone on the table. "I can't do video but is it okay if I record audio? I can use it over some setting shots."

"Rory, how many times? You are not an investigator," Leigh said, nodding to show she agreed with him recording.

"I think he has a point," I said. "Not that he should be investigating, but hearing the whole thing would help. He might ask questions we wouldn't even think about."

She sighed and then sat back as her salad arrived. Rory

moved the phone to make room for his hamburger platter, and I picked up my napkin so I wouldn't make a mess with my sandwich.

"How can it hurt?" I asked when she didn't answer.

"I can't imagine all the ways a defense counsel will use it." She glanced at the phone. "You remember the part of the agreement that said you may be called to testify in court?"

"Yeah. My dad said he'd help me out if I needed to. He won't be defense on this because I'm here, right?"

"Yes," Leigh said. "Okay, if we give you the details from the file, it increases the chances you'll be called. You won't be able to film what happens in court. And the judge might decide everything you heard and saw is privileged in some way and stop you from distributing your work."

Rory grinned. "Hey, that would be the best publicity for my next project. A rep for getting to the truth is awesome. Dude, Netflix might fund me."

Leigh shook her head like she couldn't believe his optimism. "Okay, we have that on record. Let's start with the Sandhu case." She pointed to me and took a bite of her food.

"Stabbed in Pacific Spirit Park. We know from the file that he was running and the people who found him remember seeing him before. He had a list of clients who needed reputation repair, but not who...we'll close that gap now that we have the files. We learned today he lived in Surrey but spent his time elsewhere. I got the feeling from the sister it was about image, Surrey's image."

"He was killed by someone who knew exactly what to do, someone with access to sharp knives and trained to disable first. He doesn't fit the profile of the usual death of men his age, or of stabbing victims," Leigh added. "I think that's all. Any case breaking questions?"

"I wish," Rory said. He was picking the last few fries off his plate. I was barely through half my sandwich. "I wonder how he came into contact with someone like that. It sounds like a professional hit."

Leigh made a note in her book. "Good point. I stand corrected. The idea might not break the case, but it gives us something to look into."

"Mary Copp," I said. "She lived a quiet life, worked night shift at a small call center, walked around the seawall, no hobbies as far as we can tell. Few friends. One sister. My impression is she was comfortable with herself and didn't make an effort to gain friends. We learned she could be absorbed by an interest. I didn't get the vibe it was a major problem, but it is something."

"Why would someone toss her over the edge of the seawall?" Rory asked. "Like what did she do to make someone that angry?" He looked up and saw the expression on Leigh's face. "I'm not blaming her, don't get me wrong. But unless some crazy person is tossing people off the seawall at random, there must be a connection. And no one else has been attacked, right?"

"We need to keep digging," Leigh said. "Your idea is good, and that is how the investigation gets going. Maybe we've all been ignoring the fact that it was only luck she didn't die. I guess I keep hoping she'll wake up. The other cases are more permanent."

I felt a bit of guilt about that. Leigh wasn't the only one who saw Mary Copp as less a victim of attempted murder and more a pending assault investigation. If we kept hoping she'd wake up and tell us who attacked her, the case might be too cold to close when she did, or she might die. "Someone must know her well enough to help," I said.

"We'll check it out," Leigh said as she snatched one of

my fries. "There were things in the house which might help us find someone, maybe pictures or..."

"Too bad address books went out of style," I said.

"What about the Tripton guy?" Rory asked.

"We have some leads," Leigh said. "That file was the most complete. We have interviews and reports and photos. But what we learned yesterday about Tripton's history was new. We'll follow up on what Richards told us."

WHEN WE GOT BACK to the station, I tried calling Althea O'Brien, but only got the housekeeper. Apparently, Ms. O'Brien was away until tomorrow. The housekeeper couldn't make an appointment for us but took a message. I wasn't ready to sit around for another day while we chewed on the little facts that dripped into our laps.

"We should go to Calgary," I said. "Surprise her. Maybe we'll find other leads there."

"Cool," Rory said. "Location shooting."

Leigh glanced at Kardozian's office. "We need permission, and someone to give the Calgary PD a heads up."

"Okay." I headed for the sergeant's office. "How long should we go for?"

"Don't get excited," Leigh said. "There's no guarantee she'll approve the budget. And she might only let me go."

I guess being a consultant and a filmmaker meant we were on our own when it came to expenses. "I don't mind paying for my own flight," I said. "I can probably stretch to Rory's, too."

"I can deal with that," Rory said. "I can write expenses off anyway."

Kardozian was in her office, on the phone, like it was her job to take all the calls. Remembering our last conversation, I realized it was her actual job. She waved Leigh and me in, holding a hand up when Rory moved forward. Then she turned her back to us and kept talking quietly into the handset.

I looked back at him. It wasn't fair for her to just cut him out. That couldn't have been part of the agreement.

The sergeant ended her call and turned.

"Rory should be in the room," I said. If he didn't feel ready to stand up for himself, I'd take on the job.

"It's okay, Charity," he said. "Should I close the door?"

"Hold on," Kardozian said. "Rory, come in and stand in the corner. I wasn't keeping him out permanently, but I can't have him here when I'm talking about other cases."

I felt my cheeks flush. I guess I hadn't quite gotten over the idea the cops were the enemy. Rory was better at this than I was — everyone was better at it than me.

"Are you ready?" Kardozian asked him.

"Go ahead," Rory said. "Pretend I'm not here."

She grimaced as if that was the last thing she could do.

"What did you want?"

I deferred to Leigh.

"We found a possible lead on the Tripton case," she said. "We interviewed Harvey Richards. He gave us the name of Tripton's old fiancée."

"And?"

"She's in Calgary. I think it would be most effective if we went in person to talk to her." Leigh leaned forward. "I want permission to fly there for a couple of days to question to her and follow up on Tripton's past."

"Three of you?" Kardozian asked. "The budget won't support the expense without more than just a name. Have you tried a phone interview first? If you had something concrete, maybe."

Leigh pulled back. I could tell she was going to take no for an answer, and I wasn't ready to stop fighting.

This is about solving the case, I thought as I started to talk.

"We probably won't get anything concrete unless we go to her," I said. "It's too easy for her to fob us off that way. You know face-to-face is better."

"I have to think about the downside," Kardozian said. "What if she doesn't have anything useful? Then you've wasted time and money for nothing."

"Sarge, that's not true," Leigh said. "You know closing a line of questioning even without advancing the case is important."

"You could do that on the phone or ask someone on the Calgary force to do the in-person interview."

Why is she pushing back?

Kardozian's phone rang. She glanced at it and sent the call to voicemail. "Anything more?"

"We met with Mary Copp's sister, and we visited Alex Sandhu's parents' home. They're away, but his sister gave us some depth to the profile we've started. The hottest lead is in Calgary. The others can wait a few days."

Leigh glanced at Rory and that made me wonder how the conversation would have gone if it wasn't being recorded.

Before any of us marshalled more of an argument, Kardozian's office door opened. I turned to see Cecilie Hargreaves standing there in red leather pants and a white cashmere sweater, carrying a purse the size of a small building.

"If you are all just sitting around chatting, how will you solve my dear husband's murder?" She said the words like a grieving widow, but her eyes were narrow and mean.

Chapter 15

"Why are you bothering my old friends?" Cecilie asked as she brushed past Rory to stand behind my chair.

I considered ignoring the implication that I should relinquish my seat, but since she hadn't noticed Rory's camera, I didn't want to chance her seeing it and demanding he leave. So, I stood and made a production of offering my seat.

"Detective?" Kardozian asked.

"Which friends do you mean?" Leigh asked. "We've been conducting interviews so we can find the person who killed your husband."

"Dear Harvey. He called me and said that you accused him of the crime." She slipped her purse on the desk and pulled out a handkerchief. "He couldn't possibly have harmed Jackson."

I wanted so badly to show her the recording of the interview. There was no way Harvey had contacted her, but maybe someone in his office had. She couldn't be making it all up.

"Sergeant, may we discuss the ongoing investigation?" Leigh didn't appear to have any worry about antagonizing Hargreaves. "It's against policy, and likely to damage the investigation, but..."

Kardozian reached into her drawer. "We will need you to sign an agreement not to discuss what you hear with anyone, not the press, not your current husband, not your friends."

"I don't keep secrets from my husband," Hargreaves said, dabbing at her overly made-up eyes. "And the press might help. Shining a light on the problem could bring clues in. Or do you prefer to work in the dark?"

She couldn't stop herself.

The form went back into the drawer. Kardozian placed her hand on the desk as if bracing for a blast. "We will not share information," she said. "However, I understand you are still grieving, even though you remarried. You need closure, am I right?"

"Yes. I can't really move on with my career until I know Jackson is resting peacefully." Another dab at her eyes and then the dry handkerchief went back in the bag.

"Detective Andrews, did you make an accusation?"

Leigh glanced at Rory, but Cecilie didn't seem to notice. "No, we have no reason to accuse anyone at this point."

"Is that clear enough?" Kardozian asked Cecilie.

"Well, if you haven't found a suspect, what have you been doing?"

Leigh looked like she was going to answer, but the sergeant spoke first. "That is part of the investigation, and since you insinuated you will not keep information confidential, we cannot discuss anything with you."

"I'll sign your form." Cecilie reached out her hand.

"That is no longer an option," Kardozian said. "It would only take a small slip on your part to destroy any chance of prosecuting the guilty party."

"You cannot keep this from me. Who is your superior?"

"I report to Staff Sergeant Brown."

"Then I will speak with him and we will see what you will and won't tell me." Cecilie stood, swept us with a haughty glare, and strode out of the room.

"Dude, that is some crazy lady." Rory lowered his camera. "Is it okay if I keep the footage?"

Kardozian laughed. "I may need a copy of your interview with Richards and that video before she backs down. Don't lose it."

Leigh stood. "About Calgary?"

"I still can't pay for all three of you to fly. I can cover a couple of nights in a hotel if you keep it reasonable."

"I'll see what flights we can get," Leigh said.

I followed her out of the office. "Hold up. Let's make sure we're all set to go so you book the right flight." I wasn't planning on jumping on a plane unless I had a change of clothes and a few other things. "Rory, how long will it take you to pack up?"

"Yeah, my stuff needs special packing. I need like, an hour if I leave now, and if you guys pick me up on the way."

"That timing works for me," I said. "I'm farthest away, so I should pick everyone up."

Leigh was texting, but she looked up when I poked her arm. "Oh, I just made arrangements. I can be ready by that time. Is it okay if I book a flight for around five? That will land us into Calgary around eight. Too late to do anything, but we can start early tomorrow."

Rory began packing his stuff in bags. As I watched, I

realized how much he'd been settling in. Two jackets, a couple of half-eaten bags of chips, and a pair of cargo shorts.

"Call me when you're on the way," he said. "I'll let Val know we'll be gone a few days?"

"Hold up," Leigh said. She'd been looking for flights while I'd been watching Rory. "We can't get a flight until tomorrow mid-morning."

"That's a lost day," I said.

"The only flight I could find today was seven hundred each," Leigh said. "I can't afford that."

Me neither.

"What about driving there?" I asked. "If we leave soon, we'll be ahead of rush hour out of the city. We'll get there late at night, but we just need to check in. It lets us stay as long as we need."

"Road trip. I'm in." Rory lifted the four bags of stuff he'd packed. "Can Val come?"

I didn't want to be stuck in a car with the two of them for twelve hours. "Can she leave her job for a few days?"

"I guess not. I just wanted to tell her I asked." He grinned.

"Let's keep it to the three of us," Leigh said. She looked at what Rory held. "And let's try to travel light. My car is the best for the trip, but there isn't room for a lot of luggage."

"Okay, but I'll be in charge of car snacks. I don't want to be stuck with healthy stuff."

"Can you drive?" I asked, already planning the shifts.

"Yeah. I've never done a road trip though."

"We'll figure it out," Leigh said. "Let's not waste time. Rory, we'll text when we're close. Charity, I'll pick you up as soon as I can."

We waited until Rory left and then I turned to Leigh. "Healthy car snacks? Who does he think we are?"

"I'll make sure we have some fruit and water to counter the junk food for us oldies, but we'll stop to eat. I'm not driving straight through without a break." She told me to get going as she grabbed her briefcase and started loading in the files.

Chapter 16

The trip to Calgary took a little less time than we expected because we managed to miss rush hour and cruised through the numerous construction sites that were shut down for the day. I hoped the same would work for the way back, but experience told me no matter the actual time, the trip home took forever in subjective time.

At the end of the journey the car was quiet. It turned out we all had very different ideas of what should happen on a road trip, and that made for a lot of bickering.

We called Althea O'Brien but got her voicemail. Leigh hung up. "We get to surprise her."

She answered the door when Leigh knocked the next morning. She was tall and athletic, long black hair swinging behind her in a ponytail, gym clothes, and a towel over her shoulder.

"Sorry to drop in without calling," Leigh said after we introduced ourselves and Althea ushered us into the living room of her huge apartment.

"Don't worry about it," she said. "I wasn't looking

forward to working out anyway. I'll get back to my routine tomorrow."

She didn't look like someone who missed a workout. "You know why we're here?" I asked.

"Yes, Harvey Richards called to let me know. I got the message yesterday when I arrived home. It was hard to hear that Jackson was murdered. Even now, I'm still not quite over his death. I know I should move on, but I guess you never really forget a first love."

"No," Leigh said. She nodded to Rory and added, "We'll be filming the interview if you're okay with it. We have a release form."

I didn't know why Leigh was interrupting the flow. I would have gone in for details on Althea's feelings and suspicions. But Leigh was running the interview, she'd been quite clear on that at breakfast.

"So, it's not just for the case," Althea said as she read the release. "If you make this documentary, young man, I expect two things. First, I expect to approve what you show with me in the scene."

Rory stopped recording. "I can't make promises. The cops have first say."

"I understand, that shouldn't be a problem. The second is that you talk to me when you're ready to distribute. I know some people who may help."

"Okay... uh... thanks," Rory flushed with emotion, turned the camera back on, and fussed with the settings. He had one thing on his side you couldn't learn: luck.

"Coffee?" Althea asked.

"Please," Leigh said.

Rory said he needed his hands to work the camera. I nodded and expected Althea to call her housekeeper to bring refreshments.

"I'll be back in a few minutes." She strode to the kitchen.

"Shouldn't we get our answers and go home?" I asked.

"I want her a bit off kilter. I'm worried she's rehearsed a story, and we won't get past that."

"Are you going to grill her?" Rory asked.

"I won't do it for the camera," Leigh said.

"I know," he said. "You made that clear in the car yesterday. You won't help me make a better film by screwing up your case. Message received."

I ground my teeth. The argument filled the car with frustration all the way through Banff National Park.

"Good," Leigh said, then turned to me. "Are you ready to take the notes?"

I held up the pen and notebook. "Is this prepared enough?" Okay, so maybe I was hanging onto a few of the conflicts from the drive.

"Can you be professional?" she asked.

Before I could respond, Althea came back with a tray carrying three coffees and assorted milks and sugars.

"What exactly do you want to know?" Althea asked as soon as we were settled.

I started to take notes while Leigh asked questions.

"Mr. Richards thought you might have some information from Mr. Tripton's past."

"I knew Jackson for about five years before we got engaged. I may be able to put you in contact with some old friends, but Jackson didn't keep in touch. And there weren't many of them to start with."

"You were engaged, and then it was called off," Leigh said. "Can you tell us why?"

"I don't see how that would help with the murder," Althea said. Her face paled and then two red spots flushed her cheeks. "It was a long time ago. Jackson built a new life in Vancouver before..."

"We don't know how anything will help until you tell us. It might explain some things that happened just before he died." Leigh managed to imply we were clarifying information we had. "If it's not relevant, we won't put your answer in the file. Rory can stop recording if you like."

Althea glanced Rory's way as she considered her next words. "No need to do that," she said. "It was difficult at the time, and I haven't talked about what happened. I'm just surprised at how much it still hurts to say."

"Take your time," Leigh said.

I doodled in the notebook while Althea found a tissue and clasped it in her right hand. She tried to speak a couple of times and then took a deep breath.

"We were happy," she said, barely above a whisper. "Helena, Jackson's sister, the sweetest girl, and his only family. Then, two days before the rehearsal dinner, she took ill. We rushed her to the hospital, but it was no use. She'd taken something, a poison, cyanide. They said it must have been in the chocolates we gave her."

Two poisonings in one family?

"Was there a police file?" Leigh asked.

"A coroner's inquest, but they didn't find anything to prove it was more than a horrible accident." Her words caught on a sob. "Helena had an old-fashioned photo developing room. It was her hobby, working with different exposures and treatments. They think the chemicals she used got on her hands and she tainted the chocolate. But she was so careful, I couldn't believe she'd made such a silly mistake."

"I'm sorry you have to talk about this." Leigh reached over and pressed Althea's hand in sympathy.

"Jackson and I fought about it. I wanted to keep forcing

the investigation. I went to the police, but they thought I was mad with grief. That woman took his side, she agreed we should move on, that nothing would bring Helena back."

"That woman?" Leigh asked.

"Cecilie Hargreaves. Jackson was her manager. She had one song on the radio and wanted more."

I knew there was something off about the widow.

"Were you the only one who thought her death was suspicious?" Leigh asked.

"Yes," Althea said. "At first, people rallied around, but they lost interest as time passed."

I wanted to know if there was a reason Althea took it harder than the brother. I'd promised to keep my questions to myself and I didn't want Leigh pissed at me again — who am I kidding, more pissed.

"I'm sorry," Althea said, dabbing at her eyes. "Talking just brings back everything. Her death, Jackson breaking off the engagement, the way the medical examiner and the police ignored me."

"We should go, but I don't want to leave you like this. Is there someone you can call to be with you?" Leigh asked.

"My housekeeper will be here soon. Don't worry about me. Just find out who killed Jackson. I can't help Helena, but Jackson shouldn't be forgotten."

"Perhaps you can give us the list of friends before we go?" Leigh said.

"Of course," Althea said. Her distress had faded as she spoke; now she was all business, like someone turned a tap and the tears dried up.

"Let me get my phone."

I watched her walk away until she turned the corner, the sound of her footsteps changing as she ran upstairs.

"She keeps her ex-fiancé's friends in her contacts?" I asked, looking at Leigh for some sign she agreed it was as weird, as I thought.

"Not everyone wipes out the past, Charity." Leigh cocked her head, listening for Althea's approach. "Maybe she got the friends in the split?"

Maybe, but her behavior still felt off. The whole thing, from her tears and struggle for the right words, to getting her shit together again so quickly. "I guess."

We heard Althea approaching and sat back as though we'd just been waiting.

"When the police didn't respond to me, I started keeping notes. Yes, that sounds odd, but I was convinced Helena's death couldn't be an accident. I suppose I thought I could find something to show everyone I was right."

She passed the phone to Leigh. "I can send you what I have if you tell me where," Althea said. "I can't bear to think one of our friends did it, but..."

"Thanks for this," Leigh said as she typed something. "I've sent it to the right address." She handed the phone back.

"Anything else?" Althea reached for her cup. "I should get back to my day."

Leigh's phone beeped, and she checked the message. "The files have arrived. We may want to ask you some questions once we've had time to read them. I only have one more question for now, if it's okay?"

Althea gestured for her to ask.

"Who do you think killed Helena? I mean, with all the work you've done to prove she was murdered, you must have some suspicion."

"And, now that Jackson died of poisoning, you think

the same person is responsible?" Althea asked. "But I might be wrong."

"We don't know," Leigh said. "And we'll talk to the police and the medical examiner. They may start investigating Helena's case again, so you should be prepared to be contacted by the Calgary Police Department."

"Oh. That's wonderful," Althea said, her tone flat as though all the emotion had gone into her earlier reaction. "Should I tell them my suspicions?"

"If they contact you, yes. At this point, we're the only people who are on your side," Leigh said, leaning forward again. "We know you might be wrong, but you can tell us who you think killed her."

I watched Althea consider the question. Was she dredging up memories, or thinking of a suspect to give us? The fact she needed to think about it stirred my gut instincts, but nothing I'd seen felt concrete enough. I just had this suspicion she was looking for a scapegoat, that maybe she was the killer.

"Helena was a sweet girl, but it didn't mean she was meek. She had strong opinions and she was always ready to argue her causes. We didn't agree on some of the things she supported. Sometimes we fought, more of a spat really — over before it started — but there was one person who seemed to take joy in provoking Helena."

We waited out the pause.

"Oliver Frankston," Althea said. "I'm not accusing him, of course, but there was animosity. You'll find him in my notes."

"Thank you, we'll look into it," Leigh said. She started packing up to go.

"I have a question," I said. "Do you know why Harvey Richards wouldn't tell us about Helena? I mean he was close to Jackson and I find it odd he didn't tell us about her dying in a similar fashion."

"Harvey and Jackson were not close at the time," Althea said. "Helena had been away for years, living in Europe somewhere. I think Harvey connected with Jackson a while after Helena's death, maybe six months. By then, Jackson wouldn't talk about his sister at all. Perhaps to keep Cecilie happy? Perhaps because it hurt too much."

"I thought they were old friends, from when Jackson was young."

Althea frowned. "No. I think they met through Cecilie."

"Are you certain?" I distinctly remember Harvey saying different. One of them was lying.

"For obvious reasons, I wasn't involved in Jackson's life before he left Calgary, but I don't recall him ever mentioning Harvey. Before Helena's death, I must have assumed he and Harvey met because of her singing career, such as it was. Harvey is a talent agent. He and Jackson became business partners."

She stood and brought an end to the interview by picking up the cups and placing them on the tray. I waited for Leigh to follow up with more questions, but she thanked Althea and told Rory to stop filming.

Chapter 17

The Calgary morgue looked much like the one in Vancouver and smelled exactly the same. It wasn't in the basement of a hospital. That meant we didn't need to meet with the medical examiner off site to be comfortable. He had an office away from the business functions.

We didn't sit at his desk; the chairs were set up in a conversational grouping in front of a window with a view out over the city. Bryan Coldwell was in his sixties if the lines on his face were any indication of age. He had the kind of gray skin people who spend too much time indoors get as they age. It didn't help that he probably hadn't shaved in a week and white stubble only highlighted the sickliness of his complexion.

"I did remember the case when you called, but not enough to assist you. Our files are not all computerized and Helena Tripton's isn't considered high priority; we didn't expect to look at it again."

"Does that mean you can't help us?" I asked. Leigh had deigned to let me talk as much as I wanted as long as it was clear she was the only official presence. "We were hoping for some small detail which didn't seem important at the time."

"Oh, no don't worry. Someone will be delivering the file in a few minutes. I just haven't had a chance to review the notes." He rubbed his hand through his thinning hair. "I have difficulty remembering even the most sensational cases these days without checking the facts."

"But you did remember it a little," Leigh said.

Rory moved angles and we all glanced at him. I'd become so used to his filming that he faded into the background most of the time. "Ignore me," he said.

"Yes," Coldwell answered. "I remember the case because of the woman, I can't recall her name off the top of my head, it will be in the file. She kept pushing for me to find the death suspicious."

"Althea O'Brien?" I said.

Coldwell nodded.

"Was there any time when you thought she had a point?" Leigh asked.

"No. The death was clearly an accident. I found developing fluid on her hands. Those contain multiple toxic compounds. The investigators found bottles in the dark room, broken on the floor. They said it was like she flew into a rage, but the seizures at the end would explain the destruction. In a small room like that, it would be easy to cause a vast amount of damage."

"They found her in the darkroom?" I'd kind of assumed she was discovered in her house, but I don't know why.

"Oh yes," Coldwell said. "She'd been dead about twelve hours when her brother found her."

The door opened after a discreet knock and a woman handed Coldwell a file.

"Thank you, Daphne," he said. When she closed the

door behind her, he continued, "If you will bear with me a moment while I scan the contents?"

Leigh sat back and watched as he flipped through the few pages inside. I stared out the window at the city. Watching someone read didn't feel like a productive use of my time.

"Yes, here it is." He removed a page of notes. "Althea O'Brien. That's her. She had no standing in the case, but she was persistent. There was nothing in the autopsy to support her suspicions."

"When did she stop pushing her theory?" Leigh asked.

"I'm sorry to say that we had to resort to a restraining order. It seemed to bring her to her senses and I never heard from her again."

Leigh held out her hand. "May I look at the file?"

He held out a second folder. "Oh, this is a copy for you," he said.

"Can I see the original?" Leigh asked. "My sergeant will expect me to check the copy is complete."

He handed her the file. "If there's a chance the case will be reopened, I would rather keep it."

Leigh compared the documents and then nodded. She added the copy to the contents of her briefcase and gave back the original "Thank you for your time. We'll get out of your hair."

"You will let me know if something comes of this?" He pointed to the file. "I'm confident I didn't miss anything, but...new information can change interpretations."

"I will," Leigh said. Then she stood and held out her hand to shake.

"You didn't say what prompted your inquiry," he said as he shook her hand.

"We don't want this connection getting to the press,"

Leigh said. "Her brother died of poisoning in Vancouver. I'm investigating."

"Cyanide?"

"Aconite."

"Hmm. I guess that is enough to change the interpretation. I'll contact you if I see anything that changes my findings."

Chapter 18

We drove as far as Golden, BC before we stopped for food. The conversation in the car hadn't led to any flashes of insight that pointed to the killer. Without the files to look at, questions went unanswered and Leigh wouldn't bite on any of my guesses.

Our order arrived fast and hot. Burgers, fries, and salads with non-alcoholic drinks all around. Rory's camera focused on our table, his phone recording the conversation as back-up.

As soon as we were sure the waitress wouldn't be dropping by again, Leigh put the file on the table, and we started reading the notes. She didn't comment when I passed the first one to Rory.

"Gross," he said, taking a huge bite of the burger. "I would not want to die that way."

I'd forgotten the pictures and the details in the file. Not exactly appetizing. My hunger made me keep eating as we looked. Hunger, and I couldn't let Rory think he was stronger than me.

"I'm sure if Val decides to kill you, it will be fast, and you'll see her coming," I said.

"I try not to make her too mad at me," Rory said.

Leigh passed me another sheet of notes. "Val won't kill you, she'll just disappear."

"Dude, losing her might kill me."

There was nothing in the notes that let us pin the murder on anyone. Dr. Coldwell was right about the new perspective. It must be hard for him, knowing now the death should have been ruled a homicide. I tried not to wonder how he'd missed the clues, or judge him for it.

"Another wasted day," Leigh said as she finished reading the last sheet of paper. "You guys can look them over, but I don't see anything that will help."

"If I wrote this as a movie," Rory said, "the answer would be easy. Like having no clues of who did it means anyone could be the one. And I would make a twist ending. People love those."

"We can't make this up," Leigh said. "It's not a story. Someone committed the crimes and we can't just pick a murderer and go with it."

"Rory has a point," I said. "If we have nothing to go on, why not speculate?"

"I don't want to become fixated on someone because we decided they were guilty."

"But that is exactly what we'll do when we find some-one," I said.

The waitress came by and took our empty plates, offered dessert, and took coffee orders when we declined pie.

"We need to get back to Vancouver," Leigh said. "Our case is Jackson Tripton, not Helena. Dr. Coldwell will take her file to the Calgary PD if he thinks they need to investigate."

"But what if it is connected?" Rory said. "I thought cops didn't believe in coincidences?"

"Coincidences happen all the time." Leigh dug through her briefcase, finally pulling out a pad of foolscap. "I don't want to sit here all night, but you've convinced me. Let's speculate. Who wants to go first?"

"Just the Tripton cases?" Rory asked.

"Yes," Leigh said. "Nothing indicates the others are anything but single crimes."

I sipped my coffee and waited for Rory to start.

"Okay, let's say both Triptons were killed by the same person. Who do they have in common?" He didn't even pause for breath to let us answer. "Althea. She's in Calgary, so easy to kill Helena. Vancouver isn't that far for her to go. She's the jilted fiancée, so there's gotta be some anger issues."

"But why?" Leigh asked as she made notes. "We need a motive."

"Helena was trying to split them up?" I suggested. "I also got the feeling Althea couldn't actually experience the emotions she displayed. Like she'd read about how people grieve and had practiced in the mirror."

Leigh chewed her lip and then drew some lines between the names on the pad. "There was definitely something off about her, but why would she keep trying to make the police investigate the death as a murder if she killed Helena?"

"I didn't say it was perfect," Rory said. "Maybe she knew there was nothing to support her and that meant she was safe to act innocent. But yeah, it doesn't explain why she pushed them so far that they needed a restraining order." He cocked his head like he'd heard a voice. "You think it was like a love triangle situation? Maybe Althea was hot for Helena and killed her when she wasn't up for it?"

"Seems like an overreaction to kill someone," I said.

"Okay, it's not completely out there. We'll put aside the murderous lesbian lover part for now." Leigh wrote another name on the pad. "What about Harvey Richards?"

I couldn't see him finding the backbone to kill even once. "He didn't really know Jackson when Helena died."

"He lied to us," Leigh said. "Or, Althea did."

"So that's a thing, right?" Rory sat up and pointed to the pad. "Lying to the cops is suspicious."

"Everyone lies," Leigh said. "But yes, we'll find out who was telling the truth."

"I can't think of a motive," I said.

"Dude, it's not that hard. Let's say Harvey and Jackson were planning to go to Vancouver and Helena was against the move. Harvey shuts Helena up. Then he and Jackson get rich."

"Why would he kill Jackson, then?" Leigh asked. I could tell she was getting into the guessing game.

"Maybe Jackson planned to split," Rory said. "Cecilie wanted a bigger name for an agent? People who want to be stars are always looking for the edge."

"So why not kill Cecilie?" Leigh asked.

"Maybe he tried," Rory said.

"Too many maybes," I said. "What about Cecilie?"

"Just because we don't like her doesn't make her a murderer." Leigh wrote the name down anyway.

"Her motives are obvious," Rory said. "She wanted Jackson, so she killed the sister who didn't want them to get married. We probably need to find that out. And she killed Jackson because her new husband can move her career faster."

"That's cold," I said. I couldn't argue with him. My time with Jake when he acted on shows in Vancouver stripped away any innocence I had about how the film industry worked. I was beginning to see the music industry wasn't that different.

"Okay," Leigh said. "Finish your coffee, we need to get on the road. I'm sorry I fought you on this. We've got some work to do tomorrow."

Chapter 19

The next morning, Leigh and I were in the office. Rory hadn't shown up yet, but it was six thirty and he was probably still flaked out.

We couldn't both enter information in the files, and Leigh knew the jargon, so she typed, and I sat there bored. I got why we had to do the admin stuff as we went, but I didn't like the feeling we were standing still again.

I flipped through the Sandhu file, trying to do what we'd done yesterday; I guess that needs more than one brain because no motive came to mind.

When I opened the Copp file, the contents brought back the suspicion everything was connected to the LaSalle murder.

Leigh was focused on her notes and there was no one else around. I know I promised, but when your gut won't shut up, you're better off following the feeling.

I wouldn't be able to break into the office without alerting Leigh. The only slight success I'd had was when I brought coffee. At least Detective Grewal had spoken to me when he took the drinks.

"I'm going on a coffee run," I said, grabbing my wallet. "What do you want?"

Leigh didn't even look up from the screen. "Just black, thanks."

"Back in a bit."

The coffee shop was a block away and even this early it was busy. I picked out some pastries and got enough coffee for six people. That was all I could manage to carry. By some miracle I didn't drop or spill anything until I got to the elevator. With my hands full, I couldn't call the car. Pushing the button with my elbow didn't work; elbows are too big to fit.

"Morning," someone said and reached around me to press the up button.

"Thanks," I said, turning. "Oh, hi."

It was David Anchor, and he seemed happy. "I got these for your team."

"I'm not letting you into the room. Paul would kill me and remember, he knows how to avoid getting caught." He took one of the trays off my hands. "But I appreciate you changing tactics to bribes."

"We made some progress yesterday. It made me feel generous."

The elevator arrived, and Anchor waved me in, then pressed the button for our floor.

"That can happen," he said.

"You seem happy today," I said, hopefully.

"We finally learned what she was investigating, if you can call it that." The door opened. "Nothing connected to your case," he said, following me out.

"Too bad. We're stuck, and a lead would be useful. What story was she working on?"

He sighed, the kind that ends in a groan of frustration. "If I tell you, I want two promises."

"Whatever it takes." I couldn't believe he was going to share.

"First, you tell no one. We can't have the details leak out."

"I swear. Can I tell Leigh? If she promises too?"

"Yes, you can tell your partner. She's a cop, I don't need her promise."

"And the second thing?"

"You swear you'll leave us alone." He looked around. "Paul might kick me off the case if I screw up."

How could I say yes? I know promises get broken all the time, but I liked to think that when I make one, I intend to keep it.

"That's kind of blanket," I said. "What if we find something connecting the cases? You want us to keep you in the dark?"

"No. You tell the sergeant and she'll tell us when it's not interrupting our flow."

"Okay, I swear I won't interrupt your flow."

"That's not what I asked."

I laughed. "I promise to leave you and your team alone. I promise if Leigh and I find anything we'll take it to Sergeant Kardozian."

We were standing outside the locked war room. He put the tray of coffee on a desk and unlocked the door, then picked up the coffee. "Are the pastries for us, too?"

I took Leigh's cup and mine off and handed over the bag. "So?"

"LaSalle was digging into a rumor there's a serial killer working the area. She didn't make any notes that we've found, but we will. She should have brought it to us in the first place; amateurs aren't prepared for the risks."

He slipped inside the office before I could ask anything more. He turned before closing the door. "Next time you do this, we should grab a coffee together, outside the station."

Chapter 20

Did he think of me as an amateur? I've faced off with gang members and corporate psychos; I knew the risks.

"What did he say?" Leigh asked as I returned to the cubicle with her coffee.

"He told me I didn't know what I was doing."

"That seemed to take a long time," she said, sipping her drink. "Did he say it in the elevator, or after you gave him his bribe?"

"What is with you guys and bribes? I just bought them coffee." I pointed to hers. "You think that's a bribe?"

"Touchy," Leigh said. "Is that all he said? He's right, amateurs get hurt when they try to do our job. But you aren't an amateur, so what did he actually say?"

I guess if Leigh thought I knew what I was doing, it was enough. "LaSalle was tracking a serial killer. Grewal thinks it means our cases are not linked, but I don't think he's right."

"Did David mention anything about the RCMP?"

"Dude, is the RCMP involved? That will make my documentary better. Do you think they'll work in their dress uniforms a bit?" Rory placed his camera and various other equipment on the desk next to Leigh's.

"It's not our case," Leigh said. "And no. Would you work in this weather in a heavy jacket and pants?"

"I guess I'm stuck with you two," he said, then ducked as I threw a napkin at him. "Don't worry, I'm gonna make you stars."

"So, what's next?" I asked. "We look into the backgrounds of our list of suspects?"

"I'm putting together a report for the sergeant. If she's convinced, we'll go digging before we start the questions. Talking her into it is going to take a while and I don't expect her in for at least an hour. I have an idea for you if you'd rather not sit around."

"What's the idea?" I wasn't going to agree to anything blindly.

"Last night, I wondered if we did a good job of looking through Mary Copp's place."

"There wasn't much to see," I said.

"No, but with her sister there, I didn't want to knock on walls or look for trapdoors."

"Cool, you think she was hiding something?" Rory asked.

"I don't know, and that's the problem. If we missed something, it could be important. If you and Charity want to do a thorough search while I go through the process here, it will at least close one hole in our information."

"Don't I need a warrant?"

"Lila said we could access all we want. Don't break anything we'll have to pay to fix. If you think we need to do a destructive search, we'll get a warrant and a team. Both of you wear gloves, just in case."

"I'll record everything," Rory said. "So no one can blame you if something goes wrong."

"Nothing will go wrong," Leigh said, glaring at me. "Do we agree on that?"

"I won't do anything I shouldn't. If we find something, I'll call you for instructions. I can't control the universe, but if something goes wrong it won't be my fault."

"Okay, that will have to do," Leigh said, then told me how to access the house.

"Ah, Officer Andrews," a male voice cut into our conversation.

I turned to see Ernie McBain, Cecilie's new husband, walking toward us.

Without his wife hogging the spotlight, Ernie kind of came into focus better. One of those people who faded into the background when bigger personalities were around, he was good looking and charming. That didn't buy him any credit with me. He married the woman, and did it fast, so there was something wrong with him.

"I don't want to bother you," he said. "A few minutes of your time?"

"Let's not do this here," she said. "People will be starting work soon and it will get noisy." Leigh stood and looked over her shoulder for an unlocked room. "I'm afraid we only have access to one of the rooms where we interview suspects. Is that okay? I'll make sure no one is observing and the recording equipment is off."

McBain looked around and shrugged. "Fine."

"Would it be okay if I recorded?" Rory asked. "It won't be an official one, but I'm doing a documentary on how the police work."

McBain frowned and looked Rory up and down. "Always happy to support the arts," he said with a smile. "Will I be allowed to review the final product before you release the film?"

"Sure," Rory said.

Neither mentioned anything about having approval of the footage, and I was certain that was purposeful on Rory's part.

We settled in the interrogation room. Leigh offered water or coffee and I wanted to tell her to get on with it, the prospect of going through Mary Copp's home making me impatient to start.

"No, as I said, I only need a few minutes." McBain leaned his elbows on the table. "I'm sorry to have to bring this up, but I have to protect Cecilie at this stage in her career. We're planning a big comeback for her. It's not just that she's my wife, I would do this, and have, I suppose, for all my clients."

He paused, waiting for agreement? Or applause? Leigh didn't fill the space. I noticed his face was covered in a thin film of sweat, and he was pale.

"Are you okay?" I asked, pretty certain there would be repercussions if he passed out in the station.

"I may have a slight case of the flu," he said.

"You should go to a doctor," I told him.

"Yes, I will if I don't feel better soon. So, Cecilie is quite stressed out over this. I know she's been here and that she can be difficult."

Again, a pause.

"I don't want her to slow you down. The sooner you solve this, the sooner she can concentrate on her future."

"We want a quick resolution too," Leigh said. "But, the aim of the investigation is to find the truth, not beat the clock."

"I'm sure you're working as hard as possible, Officer," he said.

"Detective," Leigh said.

"Of course, Detective. I thought perhaps we can work out something to keep Cecilie away from here and more focused on her new songs. Something to help her feel like progress is being made."

If he thought Leigh was going to ask, he was mistaken. I could tell by the way she sat straight in the chair and kept eye contact, she wasn't in the mood to offer ideas.

"Well, to be blunt, I thought if you were to update me on a regular basis, I could act as a conduit to Cecilie. She wouldn't need to come in here when she gets frustrated."

He'd run out of words and now I was tempted to jump in, but I kept quiet. This was Leigh's thing to deal with.

"If you would wait here just a few minutes, Mr. McBain," she said, rising from her chair. "Charity, can you join me in the hallway?" She looked at Rory and shook her head a fraction.

When we were in the hall, with no camera to witness, she swore and paced across the carpet. Only a few steps, but it seemed to drain off the emotions.

"If they would both let us alone, we'd solve the case."

"I don't think that argument will work," I said. "It's not your call anyway, right?"

"No, let's go talk to the sergeant."

Chapter 21

Sergeant Kardozian was hanging her coat in the small closet at the back of her office as we entered. "What now?"

I felt it was my fault that she thought we'd done something that merited the response. But maybe she just wasn't a morning person.

"Ernie McBain. He's in room one. He has a request," Leigh said.

"He wants us to update him, so he can keep Cecilie away," I added. If Leigh wanted to draw this out, I'd be stuck here, and I wanted to head to Mary's home.

"Let's talk to him." Kardozian clipped her badge on her belt. "Where's your shadow?"

"Recording Mr. McBain," Leigh said. "We got permission, don't worry."

We returned to the room to find Rory and Ernie in conversation about the difference between a music agent and a movie agent. Rory seemed to be the one doing the explaining.

When Kardozian followed us, McBain stood and held out his hand. "Good to see you again, Sergeant."

Kardozian shook his hand once and let go. "My detectives told me what you want," she said.

So, I was suddenly one of her detectives? I hoped she just meant that as a 'we are one team' kind of thing. My future didn't include a jump into police work full time.

"Yes. I think that will help all around. I'll keep Cecilie informed and she'll stay away."

"I would prefer Ms. Hargreaves let us do our job, but we don't give updates to civilians on ongoing cases."

"I understand, but surely an exception could be made?"

This was fun to watch. He was trying desperately to hold onto the friendly and helpful persona, but the skin around his eyes tightened, maybe with the effects of the flu. He looked more like he was about to puke than someone who didn't like hearing the word no. The effort was getting to him, and it wasn't a role he played well against resistance.

"No," Kardozian said. "As I said, we would appreciate your wife simply leave us to investigate and not accuse us of harassment as we do our jobs, but the case remains confidential until solved."

His shoulders slumped as he realized there was no way around it. "Thank you for your time," he said and then just walked out.

Kardozian turned to Rory. "Did he say anything while you were alone that we should know?"

"The dude doesn't know his own business, but no, he didn't suddenly say he regretted killing anyone."

"Thanks, Sergeant," Leigh said.

"You knew what I was going to say," Kardozian snapped. "You need to learn how to say no without calling me in."

Leigh didn't take that the way I would have. She

seemed disappointed in herself. For me, it was permission to control the case. We needed to talk about it, but not now, over drinks later.

"Have you cleared him?" Kardozian asked.

"You think he killed Tripton to get with Hargreaves?" I asked. "Why would anyone want to be with her at all, let alone kill someone to do it?"

"People are weird," Kardozian said. "That's the biggest lesson I learned when I started my career. You can't assume everyone is rational; if they were, no one would need the police. What happened in Calgary?"

"I'll have a report in an hour," Leigh said.

"Just the high points now, please."

"We think there might be a connection between the two cases. Jackson's sister was poisoned; they deemed it an accident, but it's a big coincidence."

"I'll wait for the details." She left the room.

"You did the right thing," I said. "He wasn't going to take your word for it."

"I didn't even try," Leigh said. "And I'm thinking now I should have pushed him. Did you see how close he was to blowing up at the sarge? He has a temper and it's not always in his control."

"We should add him to the list of people with a motive," Rory said. "Maybe Cecilie isn't as bad as we think. Maybe he's making her come here."

"That can go in her report," I said. "We should head out to Mary Copp's. I notice you didn't mention that, Leigh."

"I learn fast," she said with a grin. "By the time I make the report, you'll be done with the search, or you'll have found something."

"One moment," Kardozian said as she opened the door. "I just got off the phone with the pathologist."

Was I ever going to get out of here?

"About Tripton's autopsy?" Leigh asked.

"No. Ron Waters, your witness to the Mary Copp attack," she said. "He's dead. Opiate OD."

"That's not going to help us," I said. "You think he was high when he called 911?"

"Charity, he's dead," Leigh said.

"I didn't mean that to sound callous," I said. "Just thinking we might have lost a lead."

Turning to Kardozian, Leigh continued, "Was there anything in the autopsy?"

"They are holding off on a manner of death recommendation," she answered. "Not enough to call it murder, but no indication he was a drug user."

"The ODs are not always from long-term use," I said. "People die the first time."

"Yes, but they aren't witnesses to a crime usually," Kardozian said. "Since he wasn't a long-time user, did you suspect anything was wrong when you talked to him?"

"No," I said. "He came across as genuine."

"Okay, there was one more thing," Kardozian said. "There were traces of poison in his system. The pathologist said there are any number of plausible explanations, but he'll keep the file open for now."

"Did he say what kind of poison?" I asked.

"Same as Tripton," she said, then stepped out of the room.

"So, we have four cases?" I asked.

"Not yet," Leigh said. "But I think we need to contact McBain and tell him to get checked out. He's sick, and if I remember correctly, he's showing signs of aconite poisoning."

We got back to our cubes and I wrote the information on Ron Waters' file while I listened to the call Leigh made.

She'd put it on speaker, so Rory's equipment could pick up the audio.

"Mr. McBain," Leigh said. "I'm recommending you go to the doctor or emergency right away."

"I'm fine, Detective," he said. "It's the flu."

"Are you nauseous?" Leigh asked, referring to her computer where she'd pulled up the symptoms of aconite poisoning.

"Yes, but that's a symptom of the flu." He sounded annoyed. I wondered why someone worrying about his health would annoy him.

"And of aconite poisoning," Leigh continued. "Numbness? Cold for no reason?"

"Detective," McBain interrupted Leigh's list of symptoms. "My wife will take care of me. Cecilie is intelligent enough to know the difference between a slight stomach bug and a serious illness. She loves me, and you simply obstruct me when I try to help. Cecilie is quite capable of making me do something if she believes it's important. You worry about your business, and I'll listen to her, not you, about my health. Or are you suggesting she is poisoning me?"

"Do you think she's capable of that?" Leigh asked.

"Cecilie is capable of whatever it takes to get her way," McBain said, like he was proud of her. "But I do not think she would cross that line."

"Very well. I hope you're right about the flu, and about your wife," Leigh said. "I won't take any more of your time."

She ended the call and looked at me. "I tried, right?"

"It's all on record," I said. "There was no way he was going to take your advice."

"Okay, get over to Mary Copp's place and let me figure out how to put this in the report."

Chapter 22

I was glad for Rory's company when we walked through the door to Mary Copp's home. The house felt odd. Like someone had just left the room, but also like no one had lived there for a long time. I guess haunted was the best word.

"We'll start at the top," I said. "Put your stuff on the couch so it's all together. I don't want to leave anything here by accident."

When we were ready to search, I handed Rory a pair of latex gloves. "Hope you aren't allergic," I said. "This is all they had."

"No problem." Rory snapped the gloves on like a pro.

I somehow got the right one twisted and had to pull it off and start again.

"Should I help look?" Rory asked. "I can set up the camera so my hands are free."

My authority probably didn't pass on to Rory, but two of us looking for some faint clue seemed like a good idea. "Not by yourself," I said. "And if you find something, tell me immediately."

We headed for the bedrooms, starting with the one at the back. It was small, the closet shallow, but running the length of the wall. It made my house look large in comparison. No hatch in the ceiling. By my estimate there should've been some space under the roof, not enough for a room, but maybe enough for storage.

"Can you film me in the closet?" I asked.

"Yeah, but I'll block the light, so you'll need me to set up something so you can see, and so the camera can record more than a black space." Rory placed his camera on the window ledge, pointing toward the bed. "Search here while I figure out something I can do."

I watched as he leaned inside the narrow space. I couldn't let him go in without me, and there wasn't enough room for both of us.

He pulled back. "How the heck did she use this space? There's barely enough room to turn around. She should have knocked out the wall and expanded the room." He looked at the baseboards and then up at the ceiling. "It looks like she maybe did the opposite. I'll be back in a sec."

I unmade the bed while he left me. The mattress was whole, and no slits opened in the boxspring cambric, nor was it loose along the edges.

Rory came back into the room with a black box in his hands. "I'll set this up on the top shelf. Don't look at it directly."

"Okay." I put the bed back together and tapped my foot on the carpet. Maybe I would feel a change in the floor if there was a cutout: nothing.

"Are you ready?" Rory asked.

I couldn't think of anything else, so I nodded. He turned on the light as I slipped inside. There were no shadows to hide anything. A few rods stuck out from the wall, no hangers ready to be used. The rest of the space held shelves from top to bottom. No hatch in the ceiling, no trapdoor in the floor. The shelves weren't thick enough to have secret compartments.

"Kind of a letdown," Rory said from behind me.

I turned to answer and looked into the floodlight.

"Shit!" I closed my eyes and felt my way out of the closet. A blob of light like the sun blazed behind my eyelids. This was going to take a few minutes.

"Sorry," Rory said. "Keep your eyes shut. I'll set up in the other bedroom while you recover."

"No," I said, eyes still closed. "I can't let you be alone."

"Dude, I'll keep the camera running. I won't touch anything."

It wasn't like I could stop him. "Just lead me in there and sit me on the bed while you do your thing."

It took about ten minutes for me to recover my sight and then search bedroom number two. This one had a full-sized closet, but no hiding places. The bathroom yielded only the attic hatch.

When I opened the hatch and pulled down the ladder, it was obvious that only one of us could go up.

"Take the camera," Rory said. "You just hold it like this. Pan around the space and then do your thing."

He actually seemed to know his stuff.

I climbed the ladder one handed, putting the camera through the hatch first. I placed it on the floor because I needed both hands to pull myself through. The attic was as empty as the basement, or almost as empty. Spider webs draped everywhere.

The ceiling was too low for me to stand upright. The floor was mainly just the joists, so I backed out, promising myself to come back and search the insulation if we needed to.

Down on the main floor I grabbed a handful of paper

towels from the kitchen and rubbed my hair to get the feeling of spiders from it.

Rory was leaning against the door, looking at the corners of the room.

"Something's wrong," he said. "Wait here."

Before I got a chance to tell him to stop, he left with his camera. I tossed the paper towels and my dusty gloves. He came back as I pulled on the fresh pair.

"There's a room missing," he said. "Look."

He showed me footage of the house from the outside, just a regular mostly square box.

"I'm not seeing anything wrong," I said.

"Look around," he swung his arm in a circle. "It's not the same shape. There's a hidden room." He scanned the hall. "Over beside the stairs."

"Get filming." I walked to the wall. It was about four feet wide and covered with stripey flowered wallpaper. Before Rory's discovery, it looked normal, but now the proportion was clearly wrong. "If I can't find a way in, we'll need Leigh's permission to break through."

"No way Mary Copp would knock down the wall every time she wanted in."

Even close up, I couldn't see anything odd about the pattern on the wallpaper. A double light switch set at shoulder height seemed pretty normal; one switch for the upstairs light, and one for the front room. That way no one went to bed in the dark.

I flicked the first switch, and nothing happened. I did the same with the second, nothing again. Then, because I'm obsessive, I went back to the first and flicked it, so they were both oriented up. There was a click and a door appeared in the center of the wall.

"I need one of those," Rory said in awe. "Let's go." He took a step toward the opening.

"Hang on." A little voice inside said to call Leigh first. This was something Mary's sister didn't know about. No matter what was inside, we'd found something new in the case.

"Why? This is what we came looking for. She might have drugs in there, or maybe a body."

"Unlikely." I told the little voice we'd call as soon as we knew something useful. I took a breath and gave the door a push.

Inside was something much worse than drugs or a body. A shrine to Cecilie Hargreaves.

Chapter 23

"We need to step out now," I said.

"I could film it. Then we can study the clip later." He leaned around me and panned his camera around the small room.

"No. I think Leigh will want an official photographer. Even if she doesn't, we need to talk to her first."

I made him go ahead of me back to the kitchen. It felt like the only normal room in the house right now. I called Leigh and told her what we'd found.

"Don't touch anything. I'll call you back."

"Wait," I said. "Can Rory go in with his camera if we promise not to touch anything?"

Leigh muttered something and then gave us the okay. I realized she'd been talking to Kardozian, not muttering to herself. "Don't disturb anything. Did you pack the whole crime scene kit? Or just the gloves?"

I'd been tempted to do that when she showed me the contents of the kit, to simply grab a handful of gloves and go, but I'd been a good little detective. "You want us to put on the booties and shower caps?

"They aren't shower caps," she said. "Yes. We'll want the scene as clean as possible."

"Okay, we'll do that, and we'll film outside to see if there's anything else odd."

"I'll call you back in a few minutes, just don't screw this up."

"Yes, ma'am."

She hung up.

I turned to tell Rory the rules and burst out laughing. He was wearing one of the shower caps — I don't care what Leigh says, if it looks like a duck etc. — and the plastic shoe covers. He had a huge grin on his face and was holding out my equipment.

"Yeah, yeah. You aren't the one getting filmed looking like that," I said, taking the cap and booties.

"Untrue, and I look professional, not like a dork. I want you to record me before we go in, so no one can say I did something wrong."

"Okay. I guess Leigh's rubbing off on you." I tucked my hair in and bent for the foot covers.

Rory handed me the camera and then tucked more of my hair in. After I took a video up and down his body and made him promise that Val would receive a copy, he took the equipment back.

We stepped into the room and I acted as witness that Rory did nothing but record. He started by taking in the wall covered with pictures of Cecilie. When he was satisfied, he turned slowly to take in the whole room. It must have been another bedroom before the renovations. The space for the closet had been cleared out to hold a small table and the shrine.

Cecilie's pictures filled the niche. Some were promotional, some candid shots cut from tabloids, and some were evidently taken without her knowledge, and recently.

My phone rang as Rory moved closer and started documenting the individual pieces.

"We're on our way," Leigh said. "Ten minutes at most."

"We?"

"Crime scene techs are right behind me."

"This is linked, right? I'm not being crazy."

"It could be," Leigh said. "But we don't know what it means."

"Whoever killed the Triptons tried to kill Mary," I said. I didn't have proof, but my instinct had no doubt.

"Or, Mary killed them, and her attack was random."

"Really?"

"I'm not arguing with you," Leigh said. "We'll talk when I've seen the room."

I tucked the phone back into my pocket.

"I think I've got everything," Rory said. "You want to go outside?"

"Yes, just in case we get shut out when Leigh's people arrive."

"She won't let that happen," Rory said. "Anyway, now we have this, they can't. It backs up to the cloud automatically through my phone. My dad won't let them take that."

I wished I had his faith, but I figured the rolling wave of official process was going to sweep us away. "Okay, let's see if there are any other rooms missing."

We'd finished surveying the outside of the house when Leigh pulled up. She met us at the front steps. "We have about five minutes before the crime scene guys will send us away," she said. "We'll get their report, but they won't let us hang around."

I led her to the room. "How long before they send their report?"

"The sarge said she'd put a priority on it, but we will

still be bumped if the LaSalle case needs resources. Maybe a couple of days."

"I have it all," Rory said.

I wished he'd kept that quiet until we were gone.

"Good, that means I don't have to ask you to do a rush job," Leigh said. "No way I'm waiting for the report."

WE'D COMMANDEERED one of the side offices, brought in a monitor and computer, and spent the rest of the day and most of the evening so far watching Rory's video.

My eyes were rebelling against the hours of trying to see what each of the pictures contained. It wasn't a problem with Rory's work, there were just so many of them and zooming in destroyed the detail.

"Sorry. I can clean the shot up a bit in post, but I thought it would help more." Rory looked at his phone. "Val wants me home."

"You can go," I said. "We're not going to find anything worth filming tonight."

"How do you know that?"

He texted back to Val.

"We would have an inkling by now," Leigh said. "We should shut down and go home. Maybe I can get something from the tech team in the morning." She stretched, and I heard a lot of popping.

"Did you try calling them?" I asked. "Maybe they can give us something?"

"I doubt it," she said, picking up the phone. "But, it's not totally out of the question. We've got some visibility now, and I'm pretty sure we won't stay ahead of this after Hargreaves hears the news."

"How will she hear?" Rory asked as he started unplugging his equipment. I noticed the camera was still recording.

"It always gets out," Leigh said. She held up a finger. "Detective Andrews here. Any chance we can get our hands on some of the photos on the Copp case?"

Whoever was on the other end had more to say than yes or no. Leigh's frown made me think it was a lecture.

"Thanks," she said, not sounding thankful. "We'll be here."

"So?" I half hoped the answer was no, so I could go home and sleep.

"We should grab a bite and get some air. We'll have some of the photos in an hour. Apparently the sarge put a lot of pressure on them."

Rory started plugging things back in. "I'll go home and talk to Val, have a shower. Don't start again without me, okay?"

"We promise not to solve the case in your absence," Leigh said. "Charity, want to go for a walk?"

I stood and shook the stiffness out of my legs and back. "Sure, we need to find coffee, too."

The light in the room dimmed a little as Rory stood close to the monitor. "Dude," he said then grabbed for the remote. "Check this out."

He pointed at the picture; one we'd looked at a hundred times.

Leigh and I crowded in and squinted at the screen. "Yeah, that's Ernie, her husband."

"Right, and he's in a lot of shots with Cecilie. But here, it's just him. Look closer. The photo has been crumpled and flattened again. It's kind of hard to make out the details"

My brain was too tired to make whatever connection he saw. "Okay, so what does that mean?"

"She was angry at something," Leigh said. "If not Mary, then whoever she took it from tossed it away."

I thought we were grasping for any tiny detail. I scanned the photos around Ernie's and my curiosity kicked my brain into action. "Isn't that Althea O'Brien?"

Rory looked over my shoulder. "Yeah, and that's the Sandhu guy. And you in couple of them, Charity."

"And there's Victoria LaSalle." Leigh reached behind her for a notepad. "Hargreaves isn't in any of them."

"We need all the pictures," I said. "If she was stalking them too, it changes everything."

Leigh didn't look up from the pad. "Yeah, it could mean we lose these cases to Grewal's team."

Chapter 24

By the time we finished reviewing the photos from the lab, there wasn't any point in all of us going home for a few hours' sleep. Rory opted to leave, I think because Val kept texting, but he was young and was able to handle late nights better than we could. The break room had couches, like someone had thought of this situation but couldn't find the budget to pay for actual beds.

When Leigh's alarm went off, we washed up in the restroom. I found some gum in my purse to fake brushing our teeth and we were almost ready for the day.

"Should we both go for coffee?" I asked. "Or are you camping outside the office, so you can catch Kardozian right away?"

"She said she'd be in by seven, so we have a half hour." Leigh pulled her hair back into a ponytail and reached for her purse.

"Time for a little payback," Paul Grewal announced. He held up a tray of coffees and a bag of pastries.

"Don't you mean return the favor?" I took one of the cups and the bag.

"We'll see which one of us is right when the sarge gets here." He plunked himself on the corner of Leigh's desk. "I hear you found something we might be interested in."

I looked at Leigh, she shook her head.

"It's possible," she said. "What did you hear?"

"You mean who told me?" Grewal popped the lid of his coffee to check the contents. "Friend in the tech team. Told me you were all excited last night."

"Still our case," Leigh said. "Just because you're stuck doesn't mean you can poach."

"It's not a contest, Andrews," Kardozian said as she rounded the corner. "In my office. One of those better be for me, Grewal."

He put the last cup on her desk.

She looked over my shoulder. "Where's the kid?"

"He's not a kid," I said. "We sent him home last night. He'll be back soon."

"Then he'll miss the meeting," she said as she shucked her jacket and sat. "I'm not working to his schedule."

I got agreement to record with my phone. If Rory couldn't use the video, maybe the audio would be helpful.

"Andrews, bring us up to date." Kardozian pointed to a seat.

Leigh handed out copies of our notes. "First, Sarge, I want to be clear that this is still our case. There's nothing definitively tying Copp to LaSalle."

"Just tell us what you found," Kardozian said with a wave of her hand.

"We'll need to get all the original photos to be sure, and to see if these are part of a pattern," Leigh read from the pad. "In Mary Copp's shrine to Cecilie Hargreaves, we found pictures of Alex Sandhu, who is the victim in one of the other killings. We also saw separate pictures of Hargreaves' current husband, Jackson Tripton's ex-fiancée, and Victoria LaSalle. That's why you're here, Paul."

"Any indication that Mary Copp is the killer?" Kardozian asked.

"Since she was a victim, not at this time. We will be looking closer at her background and talking to the sister again, but there was nothing to indicate she was a danger to anyone." Leigh looked to me, her lips pressed closed.

I could take a hint, so I didn't add my theories. If she thought they were important, Leigh would ask me. That didn't stop me thinking about how I'd use them to get a look at Grewal's files.

"I need a copy of any pictures of LaSalle," Grewal said. "You might be wrong about this Mary Copp. LaSalle was looking for a serial killer, maybe your victim is guilty."

Leigh's face flushed. "You can't go fishing in our pond. We found nothing to indicate we have a serial killer on the loose."

"Maybe we just haven't made the connection because she's in a coma and the pattern is interrupted." Grewal looked at Kardozian.

"If we knew what you have, Paul, maybe we could help confirm or eliminate her as a suspect." Leigh said then turned to face the sergeant.

They both acted like teenagers looking to Mom for approval.

"Let's not forget, Mary is currently a victim," I said. "If we can't share information openly with each other, then we might miss something."

"We have to keep my case under tight control," Grewal said. "I don't see that happening with you two on board. You can't stop that woman coming here and interrupting the sarge."

Kardozian stood and slapped her hand against the

desk. "Don't respond, Detective Andrews." She waited until both of them were paying real attention and not just waiting for her to pick a side. "It is not a contest. No one is taking any cases over. Leigh, make sure Paul has any photos that are germane to his case. Paul, if you run into any information that would help Leigh and Charity, you hand it over immediately. Am I clear?"

"Yes," Paul said. "Is that all?"

"Yes, Sarge," Leigh said. "The photos should all be here this afternoon. I'll make sure there are copies for Detective Grewal and his team."

The two different responses didn't go unnoticed. "One more thing before you go back to work, Paul," Kardozian said. "Cecilie Hargreaves is not Detective Andrews' problem. She's mine. So, if you think she's not being handled correctly, please feel free to let me know."

We were outside the office before I could blink.

"Someone will be in the room when you get the photos," Grewal said.

"That got heated," I said, always willing to state the obvious.

"Yeah, sorry about that," Leigh said. "You know how easy it is to become personally attached to cases."

"I think you came out of it fine," Grewal said. Then he grinned. "I may have some hard work ahead to make up for what I said."

Chapter 25

Rory arrived an hour after the meeting. Leigh and I were elbows deep in the current files, looking for any connection to Mary Copp. Reading the information in this light revealed a few questions we wouldn't have otherwise asked.

I transferred the movie file to Rory, so he could at least hear for himself what happened in the meeting.

"I should have stayed," he said.

"You have a life to deal with," I said. "We don't expect you to work like us unattached detectives."

"Speak for yourself," Leigh said. "I'm lucky that I can make arrangements easily to handle my life. Being alone isn't always a benefit."

"I thought you were single," I said.

"I am. There are other things that complicate life."

"That Grewal guy has some balls," Rory said. "Is it usually okay to talk to your boss like that?"

"She lets them blow off steam as long as everything stays clean," Leigh said. "Cases can be frustrating; it's not always healthy to keep things bottled."

"You didn't do that," I said.

"Not that pissed off yet," she said. "Okay, we're all here and I'm not going to sit around waiting for pictures."

"I thought it wasn't a contest." I started piling files and notes together so we could read them through.

"Like hell it isn't." Leigh held up a set of keys. "We have our own war room."

Small and a bit dim, our war room was still a step up from a cubicle. We sorted the files onto the conference table. Leigh raided the supplies cupboard. There was no white board, but we could tape paper to the wall, we could write on the window, and we could lock the door. Heaven.

Rory ran to his car and came back with a tripod. "If I set up in the corner, the shot will cover the whole room. Then I can help."

I expected Leigh to remind him we were the detectives, but she surprised me.

"Good. When you're ready, start with our notes from the road. Put people's names up and link them where we found a possible motive."

"I'll put our victims on the top," he said. "Unless Mary Copp is now a suspect?"

I sorted good pictures of Mary, Alex, and Jackson to the side for Rory. "She can be both," I said. "Treat her as a victim and then we'll make the connections."

It took less than half an hour for us to fill the walls and window with information. Our three victims were linked lightly, but it was still about gut feelings.

"Do we have a picture of LaSalle we can use until the originals arrive?" Leigh asked.

I opened my official police issue laptop and sent a photo from the paper's website to the printer. Rory ran across the office to retrieve the copies as though someone might steal them.

"Ideas?" Leigh asked as we sat and looked around us.

"It looks like real cases," Rory said. "And I didn't even notice some of that stuff before."

"Visuals are always better," Leigh said.

While we were staring at the walls, the door opened, and our box of photos arrived.

"Three copies of each," the woman said. "The originals are in sealed evidence bags." Then she went on her way.

"Should we give Grewal a full set?" I asked. "We won't have to waste time pulling out the ones he needs."

"We'll pull pictures for him as we go through them," Leigh said. "We may need every copy we have. Getting more will take time."

"I can make photocopies, so we still have full sets," Rory said.

"Are you bucking for a job here?" Leigh asked.

"Not a chance, I couldn't take the rules. I'm super stoked about these cases because the documentary is going to be epic."

I flipped through my pile of photos and placed about half of them aside. Rory was culling his for Grewal after receiving specific instructions from Leigh to make sure he didn't get anything more than he needed, but not to hold back.

Leigh put her last picture on one of five piles she'd created. "Let's go back to my original question," she said. "Ideas?"

"Don't answer until I get back," Rory said. "Two minutes to photocopy and deliver."

While he was gone, I flipped through the pictures I'd discarded one more time. "What's with the five piles?"

"Cecilie official, tabloid, and stalker," she said, tapping each one. "People we know, and people we don't. How did you sort?"

"Ones I thought were useful and ones I didn't," I said. "It looks like Rory didn't sort anything other than the ones for Grewal."

"Okay, I'm back." Rory closed the door behind him and sat in front of his scattered photos, tossing the ones he'd copied on top. "Who goes first?"

"How about you?" Leigh said.

"Maybe I don't have a theory of who exactly did it," he said. "But these were taken over about a year. All of them look like they were taken here, the ones that Mary took, I mean." He waited for Leigh to nod. "So, Mary didn't just decide to stalk Cecilie recently. Maybe we'll find a clue about the murders in her pictures. And maybe the guy who threw her over the seawall is in here."

Not something I would have thought about. Maybe I should start thinking like a storyteller.

"That's good work, Rory." Leigh pointed to her files. "I think we'll find our killer in here. Mary went a long way back with her collection. The official pictures are from Cecilie's early career and I think she was a fan, but then it turned dark. I think that happened recently. Something changed and pushed Mary into obsession. Maybe she found out about Helena? Maybe Jackson's death? If she's really obsessed, she might believe she's mourning them like Cecilie does."

"You mean like she should be," I said. "I think there are links here to all the cases. Ours and Grewal's. Maybe some other murders, too. I think LaSalle might have been tracking Mary as the serial killer."

"What makes you think that?" Leigh asked.

"Right now, just a gut feeling. There are pictures of all the dead people, except Mary. No pictures of her and she's not dead as far as we know. But there are other people here. I think we should make sure they're all healthy."

"It will take a while to identify them," Leigh said. "So, you think Mary was the killer?"

"I think Cecilie is the killer," I said.

"Whoa," Rory said. "Where did you get that?"

"There's nothing here to prove that," Leigh said.

"Yeah, I said it was a gut feeling, but you can't argue that she's not connected. Her husband, her husband's sister, she's in here with two murdered people. Maybe she was having an affair with Sandhu and he wanted to end it."

"I can't take that to Kardozian."

"Can we attempt to make the connections, or are you saying no?" I'd prove it on my own time if I needed to.

"We can try," Leigh said. "We need to be quiet about what we're doing. If she finds out, Hargreaves will shut us down."

"She won't be able to if I'm right," I said.

Chapter 26

Unfortunately, our insights didn't turn into a flurry of action. It turned into a bunch of phone calls. Rory said he had enough footage of us on the phone and left to edit his files with a promise we'd call him if anything happened. I was jealous of his means of escape.

"Could we go barging in again?" I asked. "Leaving messages didn't get us anywhere last time."

"I know, but doing it this way lets us say we tried the civilized way."

"What about exigent circumstances?" I felt like kicking in a few doors. Not sure which, but sitting at the phone was getting on my nerves. It didn't help that Paul Grewal's team seemed to be onto something. The detectives were in and out of the war room, new papers going up on walls, phones ringing.

"Not an excuse to do whatever you want."

"What will it take to get us out of here?" I ran my fingers down the list of people I still had to phone. We'd pulled all the possible leads into two lists, Leigh had one and I had the other. None of the names felt good for the crimes, at least none except Hargreaves and O'Brien.

"If we get a call from the psychologist," she said. "If he tells us Mary might be capable of violence like this, we'll start kicking in doors, metaphorically. If anyone on the list answers the freaking phone, we can go talk to them right away. Believe me, I'm no happier with this part than you."

"What about going back to Harvey and asking if he can identify either of the other two?" I picked up the phone to reach out to the next person, the manager of Sandhu's gym.

Leigh looked at me over the divider between our cubes. "I thought you'd be pushing to go interrogate Hargreaves."

"Harvey was much more willing to talk," I said. "I want to save her for when we make the arrest."

"Don't become too focused on someone we can't link," she said. "If it's her, I'll be happy to make the arrest, though. The thing is, murderers come with all kinds of attitudes, so our killer could be Helpful Harvey."

"We won't find out by leaving messages," I said.

"We can't do anything until we've left all of them."

My phone rang before I could drag us further down the spiral this argument was headed into.

"Dude," Rory said, interrupting my official phone greeting.

"We don't have anything new," I said.

"I might. Can you come to my place? Right away?"

I didn't care what it was, I said yes and told Leigh we needed to leave.

I expected a lecture about process, but Leigh grabbed her jacket and followed me out.

. . .

WE WERE SITTING in Rory and Val's living room waiting for Rory to show us what he found. Val played hostess with coffee and cookies on a plate.

They lived in his parents' pool house. It was almost the size of my home, and the furnishings were better quality. A big change for Val to go from the streets to a basement apartment to what most people would call luxury. I was proud of her; like my little sister had made good.

"It's not a premiere, Rory." I dunked a cookie and sucked the coffee out before biting.

"It is for him," Val said.

Leigh, relaxed on the couch, didn't seem anxious to start. Maybe she was just happy to be out of the office.

"So, I was editing," Rory said as he joined us. "And I found something. Val thinks it's real, like, I found something to solve the case. I'll run the shots and let you decide before I tell you. Is that okay? I don't want to sway you. You guys are the investigators, right?"

"Rory isn't stupid," Val said, looking at Leigh. "He found something real."

"I never said he was stupid, Val," Leigh said. "Charity and I are experienced; Rory's job is to record."

"Maybe you'll change your mind," Val said. "Start it, babe."

When had she picked up Rory's habit of calling everyone babe? "Do you want to become a cop?" I asked Rory.

"No, dude, it's not about that. Val, babe, just let it go."

"Can we see the footage?" Leigh asked, apparently not interested in defending our expertise to Val.

Rory pressed a button on the remote and the TV came to life. "It's only five minutes," he said, pressing another button.

The screen filled with a shot of Mary Copp's street.

Then flicked to more street scenes, some of them in Calgary, nothing worth calling us over.

"What were we supposed to see?" Leigh asked.

"Nothing yet," Rory said. "Remember, I saw these at slow speed, and a lot of times because I was editing. It took me a while to catch it, too."

"Play it again, Rory," Val said. "They'll see what we did."

"First, do you recognize the scenes?" Rory asked.

"Mary Copp's place," I said. "I think one of them was outside the Sandhu home."

"And outside the coffee shop where we talked to the pathologist," Leigh said. "And when we left Althea O'Brien's place in Calgary."

"And when we left the medical examiner's office," Rory added. "Those are the important ones, but this same thing is in every scene you saw."

"Okay. Show it again. Can you slow down?" Leigh asked. She leaned forward, placing her cup on the coffee table.

"The other thing you should know," Val said, "is that these are in chronological order. So, it's not just what is in the pictures, it's when."

"Let's go," I said. This was far more interesting than leaving phone messages, even if there was no value in what they'd found.

"This version is stills," Rory said. "It might help."

The second run through was slower. Because they were photos rather than film clips, we could see everything. Rory waited each time for us to say we'd finished looking. Toward the end, we just needed a few seconds to confirm what he'd found.

"Hargreaves. She's following us?" Leigh asked.

"Checking up on us? This explains how she knew about Harvey Richards. I knew he wouldn't have called her."

"Exactly," Val said, throwing up her arms. "She's the killer, right?"

"That's a leap," I said. I know I thought the same thing, but hearing it from Val made me realize that there was no proof, and proof was the only thing that would send the murderer to prison.

"She's definitely not supposed to do that," Leigh said. "Even the press knows not to stalk investigations." She stood. "I guess we'll talk to the sergeant and get her to call Hargreaves on it."

"If she's the killer," Val said, "does that mean anyone in the photos could be a victim?"

"Maybe," I said. "Why?"

"You're in there," she said. "You might be on her list of targets."

I started to say no but realized something that made me stop. "Am I the only one of us in the shots?"

"I haven't seen Leigh or me in there yet," Rory said.

I looked at Val, who swallowed under my gaze. She was usually so confident that I forgot everyone in her life kept leaving, parents dead, sister living somewhere hiding her past. "I'll be careful," I said. "I won't eat anything she offers me."

"She doesn't just poison people," Val said. "Be extra careful."

"I promise. Now we should call Kardozian."

"No," Rory said. "I mean, there's something else I, we, thought of."

He might not want to be a cop, but something had rubbed off on Rory.

"What?" Leigh asked.

"I've had more time to think about this," Rory said.

"And Val helped. The picture outside Mary Copp's place was the first time we were there. What if that room wasn't a stalker's paradise at first? What if Cecilie Hargreaves put everything there to blame Mary Copp?"

"That's a stretch," Leigh said. "But not impossible if she's the killer. Good work, both of you."

"But she is the killer," Rory said.

"No proof of that." Leigh looked at the screen again. "Can I get a copy?"

"Sure, but what about her?" Rory asked, pointing at the photo of Hargreaves standing by a car outside Mary Copp's home.

"You can't jump to guilt," Val said. "Remember how it was when I got accused of murder?"

"Babe, it wasn't all bad. I got to meet you." He pulled a thumb drive from his computer.

"How are we going to eliminate her as a suspect?" I asked. "If she isn't guilty."

Leigh tucked the thumb drive in her pocket. "If we go at her too soon, we'll spook her — if she is guilty. We don't have enough information to be sure what the right questions are, and we have nothing to hold her. If she thinks you suspect her, she could just leave the country."

"No way," Rory said. "She's getting another chance to be famous. She won't give that up unless she's sure."

"I thought you were going to keep your mind open," Val said. "Leigh knows how to deal with this."

I noticed we'd all shifted position a little. Now we were aligned as though the arguing was about to turn into a fight. If we kept at it, nothing would get done. "So, we can't talk to her at all?"

"I need to think," Leigh said.

"Hey, sit down and think here," Rory said, pointing to

the couch. "We'll be more comfortable than that cubicle, or the conference room." He said the last with air quotes.

"I want to look at the files again," Leigh said.

"I have copies," Rory said. "Remember you sent them to me?"

"Come on, Leigh," I said. "If we stay here, we won't attract attention. Kardozian won't drop by."

"I'll order pizza," Val said. "Food is always good for thinking."

"Okay. As long as everyone agrees we don't have anything to pin on her yet." She joined me on the sofa. "Except maybe interfering with an investigation, but that's a long stretch from murder."

The tension in the room eased as we relaxed on the couch and weren't bracing ourselves for a fight.

"What kind of proof will you need?" Rory asked.

"We have to keep investigating every suspect," Leigh said. "Yes, it's a pain, but we don't have a lot of them. If we narrow down too quickly on one, the defense will point to the other suspects as reasonable alternatives."

"So, we have Cecilie and Althea?" I said.

"McBain is a good suspect too," Leigh added. "And so are people we don't even know about."

"Do we care about them?" Val asked. "I mean, isn't it more likely that the killer is one of the ones we know?"

"Let's focus on just Jackson Tripton," I said. "If we don't have enough to find his killer, we really don't have enough to tie them together. Being in a series of pictures isn't enough."

"We could call her in for an update," Leigh said. "Ask her some questions, let her lead us to what we want."

"Like, did you kill a bunch of people?" Rory asked. "Will I be able to film?"

"That's the deal," Val said. "Rory gets to record everything, right?"

"Yes, but let me warn you," Leigh said. "First, the department might not give you the okay to publish the interview, and if they do, Hargreaves might have a veto on it."

"Yeah, I know," Rory said. "You said 'first', so what else?"

"You don't ask questions." Leigh frowned at him. "You've been helpful, Rory. If we get permission to interview her, I ask all the questions. And I will only ask ones we have the answers to."

"What about getting more answers?" I asked.

"If we can catch her in a lie, we'll have something to go on," Leigh said. "If we don't know the truth, how will we tell if she's lying?"

"Okay, I'm good with that," Rory said. "When do we do it?"

"One more thing," Leigh said. "I'm not convinced. Don't start again. I get that you have a gut feeling. I know instinct is often right, but we have just as many links to the other suspects. Keep that in mind."

"Will you ask her about the pictures?" Before I agreed to her terms, I wanted more than just a 'trust me' kind of thing.

"I'll find a way," Leigh said. "And I'll ask about LaSalle, but we'll keep that to ourselves when we ask the sarge to approve the interview."

Chapter 27

When we got back, Kardozian was in a meeting. Leigh pulled me into our conference room. "When Rory gets here, keep him busy. I don't want him in the office when I ask about the interview."

"That's not the deal," I said.

"I'm afraid Kardozian won't go for this if it's on record. And I can't fight for your idea with him in the room."

"My idea?" I kind of understood that Rory was changing the game by witnessing it, but if Leigh thought of this as *my* idea, would she fight hard enough?

"That's how I'm going to present it," she said. "And before you ask, no, you won't be there."

"You can't shut me out," I said, feeling my gut tighten in anger. "You came to me, remember?"

She shook her head like she was clearing out the cobwebs. "Let me start again. I am not shutting either of you out. I'm afraid this is going to be harder than you think. Hargreaves won't hesitate to go to the press if she thinks we're accusing her. Great publicity for her career and shitty for us. I might need to use you as the scapegoat, and I can't do that with you in the room."

"You can," I said. "I'll play along."

"If you are there, we'll end up arguing over the wrong stuff. If you don't react, it will look like a setup. Can't you just trust me?"

"I want to, Leigh. But you don't think she did it," I said. "How do I know you'll fight hard enough?"

"Well, if we don't interview her now, you won't let it go, and you have Rory on your side, so my day will be filled with nagging. And I didn't say she wasn't the killer. I said we don't have enough to prove she is."

I hated not being with Leigh, but maybe it was the right approach in this organization. I'd never worked for a place with rules, so maybe I was missing some political aspect.

"Charity?" Leigh asked. "Rory's here, and Kardozian is on her way back to her office."

"Fine," I said. "If you don't get us this interview, we will make your life hell."

She laughed like I was joking.

Leigh left, and Rory turned to follow her. "Hold up," I said.

"But..." He pointed to the office.

"We need to let Leigh do her thing unobserved." I pulled him back to the war room. "Recording her fighting with her boss isn't going to be allowed into the movie." I wouldn't let that happen.

"Fine, what do we do while we wait?" he said.

"I thought you'd fight more." I started sorting the photos back into a pile.

"I can be reasonable," he said, "when you're right."

"Did we get the results of any fingerprints?" I asked.

"I'm a visual guy. I didn't look at the other stuff, yet."

If the shrine was staged, maybe we'd find something there. "Mary Copp had that hidden room for a reason," I said. "What do you think was in the room before, if it was all made up?"

"Her sister said she'd get mega focused. Maybe she had a butterfly collection." He set up his camera. "I'm filming us," he said.

"Why would you say butterfly collection? Did you have one?"

"No, my creepy cousin did. All those bugs pinned out? Who but a crazy person would do that?"

"People with mental issues aren't crazy," I said.

"Sure." He took the pictures from me. "Why don't you let me go over these again while you dig through the technical reports."

The original photos were all still in the bottom of the box, along with two files of test results.

"No fingerprints," I said. "Not even Mary's. That's something Leigh could have used with Kardozian."

"No argument," Leigh said, closing our door behind her. "Well, not a real one. We can interview Hargreaves, but it will be in Kardozian's office, and she'll be there."

"Do we get to use all our questions?" I asked.

"Yes. She just wants to make sure that if Hargreaves complains, she can give us back-up."

"Won't my recording do that?" Rory asked. He didn't look up, but I knew he was expecting to be cut out of the meeting.

"Yes," Leigh said, "but she needs firsthand knowledge to act fast."

"It's like she doesn't trust us," I said.

"You don't know what it means when someone has your back," Leigh said. "Unless we screw up completely, this is a good idea."

"It'll be crowded." I tried to picture how we'd manage in the office.

"That's a tactic," Leigh said. "No more arguing."

KARDOZIAN MIGHT NOT LET us run free, but she didn't waste time. The next morning at ten sharp, Cecilie Hargreaves and Ernie McBain were sitting in the visitor chairs in her office. Rory filmed from the corner, Leigh and I sat on folding chairs beside the sergeant.

My anger at not being able to use an interview room vanished as I realized how uncomfortable the crowding was making our suspects.

"You said we would be getting an update," McBain said. "Feel free to start. We have busy schedules."

"Before we do that," Kardozian said, "my detectives have a few questions. The answers you give will inform the update."

She sounded so friendly if you didn't listen to the words. She left no wiggle room. If they refused to answer, we wouldn't give them anything. I tried to remember how she did it. If it had been me, I would have been blunt in holding the information hostage and probably piss everyone off.

"Do we need a lawyer?" McBain asked, checking with Hargreaves. He was looking a little healthier. Not completely well, but enough for me to believe it had been the flu.

"Let's just listen," Cecilie said, patting his knee like he was a fussy child. "We aren't required to answer."

Where did people go to learn how to say one thing and communicate another? I was ready to sign up. The words were comforting. The tone was pure steel.

"We have some new information," Leigh said. "It

would help to confirm your whereabouts on a few different dates."

"I will need to check my schedule," Hargreaves said, but she didn't reach for her phone to look at her calendar.

Leigh gave the dates and times when Hargreaves was seen in Calgary and outside Mary Copp's place.

"Cecilie was in Calgary for the first, so I'm sure that clears her of anything you might suspect." McBain reached for his phone and checked the calendar. "I was here in meetings with clients. The other date...Ah, Cecilie had a spa appointment."

"And your schedule for that same day?" Leigh hadn't caught Hargreaves in a lie to us, but she'd lied to her husband. At some point she would put that on the table.

"Lunch with a producer up from Hollywood." He glanced at Rory. "Actually, that might interest you, young man."

Rory ignored him.

"Do you know a woman named Mary Copp?" Leigh looked at both of them.

"No," McBain said. "I haven't heard the name."

"Ms. Hargreaves?"

"Perhaps if you had a picture?" Cecilie said. "Is she a fan?"

Leigh took an old photo of Mary out of the file and passed it to Hargreaves. "This is Mary Copp."

Cecilie barely glanced at the photo. "No. I've never seen her before."

Maybe a lie, but it was possible that Mary didn't actually contact Hargreaves.

"Alex Sandhu?" Leigh handed over a picture.

"No," Cecilie said. "I do meet a lot of people, but I don't remember this man. Honey?"

McBain looked at the photo and then at Hargreaves.

She smiled at him. He turned to face Leigh. "I don't recall meeting this person. Is he an actor or a singer?"

"We aren't aware of any interest in that direction," Leigh said.

"Is that all?" Cecilie asked. She crossed her legs and folded her hands in her lap. "I really am anxious for you to close the case."

"We spoke with Althea O'Brien. When did you last see her, Ms. Hargreaves?"

"Jackson's old fiancée? I haven't seen her in years. I barely knew her when we were in Calgary."

While she talked, McBain watched her, tensing at the denial. There was definitely something going on. Maybe he suspected Hargreaves had been in Calgary to stalk us. Maybe he didn't know whether his wife was lying or not. It looked to me like he was poised to handle a slip. It was almost like he thought Cecilie would blurt out that he was the one acquainted with Althea and make him confess to killing Helena.

"You didn't run into her when you were in Calgary?" I asked.

"My wife answered the question," McBain said, almost rising from his seat in eagerness to tell us off. "What is this about? I don't think you brought us here to give us an update. You think we did something wrong." He looked at the two pictures on the desk. "What did these people say about us?"

"Mr. McBain," Leigh said. "Please calm down. We have not accused you or your wife of anything."

"Not outright." He stood. "Come on Cecilie. We don't need to sit here. They can't keep us, and we need to talk to our lawyer."

Hargreaves didn't move. She acted like he wasn't even in the room. "Sergeant, are we suspects?"

"We ask questions of everyone involved in an investigation," Kardozian answered. "If you don't want to answer, then you may leave."

"So, there was no update?" She sounded disappointed.

"Cecilie."

"In a moment, Ernie." She turned to Leigh, then me. "Do you have any other questions?" A glint of challenge shone in her eyes. "No? Then we will leave. The next time we come, we'll bring legal counsel. And, Ms. Deacon, if you persist in this attack on my character, I will have your license revoked."

"What license?" I knew what she meant but needed her to say it.

"I hired a private investigator of my own," she said. "You rely on your investigator's license, correct? I have friends who will make sure you lose it."

They marched out, McBain with an aura of barely held in anger, and she with the air of injured innocence.

"Well?" Kardozian asked.

"She did it," Leigh said.

"Maybe her husband knows about it, or they're partners," I said. "Maybe he's just a victim she hasn't killed yet."

"If you still have maybes, you don't have a case," Kardozian said. "Find answers. The next time they come in, I want to press charges against someone."

Chapter 28

We spent the morning following up on clues, trying to eliminate suspects. Leigh kept reminding me we had to act as though each of them was the killer. Not like they were just a step on the path to arresting McBain or Hargreaves.

"I get it," I finally said. "We have nine possible killers. Three of them under the unknown category, and the rest we can follow up on."

"Dude, can you list them for the camera?"

Leigh ignored him and kept sorting papers.

"There's Hargreaves and McBain," I said. "Alone or as a team. Althea O'Brien, Harvey Richards, but both feel too peripheral to be the killer. Mary Copp, but we can't explain her attacker." I grabbed a Post-it note. "Add the guy who called in the attack to the list, Ron Waters. Maybe he tossed her and dialed 911 to throw us off the scent."

"We want to narrow it down, not keep adding names," Leigh said. She took my note and started another pile. "He's dead, so we can't arrest him."

"I count three unknowns. Mary's attacker, some rabid

fan, and just a plain unknown person." I sat down, over-whelmed at how little progress we'd made.

"This is how it works," Leigh said. "The killer is on the list. Now we start drilling into the right one."

"Fine." I held out my hand. "Where do I start?"

"We'll split McBain and Hargreaves, so we have two different perspectives." Leigh handed me McBain. I owed her a favor for saving me from Hargreaves. "If you take Althea, I'll take Harvey. And maybe we should follow up on Ron Waters' death."

"I'll take him," I said. "I'll see if the pathologist has anything to help us. You take Mary and I'll help when I clear my list."

"What about that Sandhu guy?" Rory asked.

"As a suspect?" Leigh asked. "You think?"

"No. Just seems like his case dropped off the radar. And he was in the pictures, too." Rory fiddled with his camera.

I put the documents on the table. Rory's words had hit home. We'd been so wrapped up in this one case we hadn't paid much attention to the others until Mary's shrine tied her to Hargreaves.

"Same killer?" I asked. "I know it sounds like a reach, but hear me out. He was in the pictures. If we believe the same person killed Helena and Jackson Tripton and tried to kill Mary, it's not too much of a leap to killing Sandhu and anyone else in the photos."

"If that's true," Leigh said, "and I'm not saying it is, everyone on our suspect list is also a potential victim."

"We better move fast," I said, reaching for the phone. "I'll start with the witness."

"If you split up, I only get one side of the story for the documentary. What if I'm with the wrong one?"

"We'll figure it out when that happens," I said, shuffling through the files for the number for the pathologist.

"Not a good idea," Leigh said. "You wanted to know how the police investigate murders?"

"Yeah," Rory said. His tone indicated to me that maybe he'd changed his focus.

"Stick with me. Charity can do her best to record what she's doing."

"Okay," he said, sounding disappointed.

I tried to believe it was because he wanted to follow my stellar investigative activities, but it seemed like he didn't want us to split up. I'd remind him he had a contract with the cops he needed to honor if it came up again.

I found the number and called about our witness.

An hour later, I'd scratched Ron the witness and Althea off my list. The autopsy report alibied him. He had a broken humerus and it was still healing at the time of his death. The injury would have made it impossible for him to toss Mary.

Althea had been out of town in Paris on the day Mary was attacked. The time also covered Sandhu's killing. I asked her if she'd seen Cecilie recently, and she said no. It didn't take her fully off the list for the Triptons, but if we were looking for someone who committed all the crimes, Althea was in the clear.

Leigh was still finishing up a call and Rory was texting with someone, probably Val, when I looked up from the phone. Paul Grewal knocked on the door and stepped in.

"How come you can just come in here when your room is off limits?" I was only half joking.

"That might change," he said. "Look, we're stalled and I'm starting to hear about how much my investigation is eating budget. The pressure from the media is fading with time. Can I transfer one of my detectives to your team?"

Leigh hung up the phone. "Is the sarge okay with this?"

"I'll run it past her if you're okay with it," he said. "It will lower the cost of my investigation, and you look like this is getting big enough to need help."

Unless I'd lost all sense of reading people, he was sincere. "Who are you sending us?"

"I'm not taking on your weakest person," Leigh said.

"Okay. What about David Anchor?"

Leigh nodded. "Fine, let me know when he's coming, and I'll make sure he's up to date."

Grewal left, heading toward Kardozian's office.

"Is that normal?" I asked.

"I have no idea, but if he's getting ahead of the brass complaining, then it makes sense."

"What about David Anchor?" He'd been the one to give us information earlier.

"Good detective, he'll be helpful…"

"But?" I asked.

"We need to make sure he doesn't take over the case. He's not that kind of guy, but he has experience and we don't. If we show weakness, we'll lose the lead."

"Dude," Rory said, "that will make great conflict for the story."

"That doesn't even go to the sarge for approval," Leigh said.

Chapter 29

David Anchor joined me ten minutes after Leigh and Rory went off to talk to Mary's sister again.

I was digging into Ernie McBain's past when the door opened. David was taller than me by a few inches, and lanky. He moved with the grace of a giraffe. I did like his red hair and freckles, but that didn't matter. We were here for the cases.

He smiled, and I had to remind myself again I was a professional and he was a co-worker and off limits.

I told him about the interview. "Take a seat."

"Can I check out the wall first?" He didn't wait for the answer. "You've made a lot of progress. Those cases were ready to be filed with the rest of the cold ones."

"How much do you know?" It was my job to bring him up to speed, and I didn't want to waste any time I didn't need to.

"The sergeant briefed me. You have some theories." He sat and glanced at my monitor. "Mr. Hargreaves. I thought we cleared him."

"Don't call him that in front of his wife, she might

make it permanent," I said. "We found a new angle on the three cases. McBain isn't as forthcoming as he seemed at first. I'm supposed to be looking for reasons he isn't a suspect."

"And what are you doing instead?"

"I'm not responsible for what I find," I said, then I laughed at his expression of doubt. "There's a lot here making him look suspicious, maybe not enough to make him a suspect."

"Personal or business?" He reached across me to turn the monitor toward him.

"Why does that matter?"

"Personal carries more weight," he said. "At least in this case. He works in an industry that thrives on the shifty and shady. He's good at his job if I remember the file correctly, and if all you found was business related, maybe that's just how he got to be so successful."

"I know what that business is like," I said, turning the monitor back. "I found questionable stuff on both sides."

"Like what?" He sat back and looked at me, waiting for the answer.

As I thought about what to say, Leigh's voice started talking in my mind. *Don't let him take the lead.* I'd almost fallen for his charm.

"Let's start with you telling me what details you have on all the cases and I'll fill in the gaps."

He smiled again and straightened. "Okay, fair enough. You think all three cases are connected. You've found a case in Calgary, Tripton's mysterious sister, you think is linked, and you don't believe the coma girl is a stalker."

He had the high points, so I walked him through the details and the links we thought made the case.

"The guy with the camera found it first, right?"

"Rory noticed the pictures, yes. Are you going to have a problem with Rory filming you?"

"Nope. I figure he's going to go with the person likely to find the killer, so if he's with me, that's good."

"Okay, we're down to four people still on our list of suspects. Cecilie Hargreaves, Ernie McBain, Harvey Richards, and Mary Copp."

"You think the killer is Hargreaves?" He looked at the board again. "She's pretty small. I get the poisoning, but stabbing a fit guy like Sandhu and throwing coma girl over the seawall?"

"Mary Copp," I said. "We did realize it was a stretch, but we can't afford to ignore the clues." There was one more link we'd been kept from following up on. "LaSalle is in the pictures, too."

"Can't talk about that," he said. "Who is Andrews off interviewing?"

"Mary's sister. We suspect someone staged the shrine we found."

"So, you're looking for the sister to confirm it's like Mary, or not?"

"And to get the medical records, or the name of her doctor. Ms. May was helpful to start, so it is possible."

"What do you want me to do?"

A loaded question on so many levels. "When Leigh gets back, we'll figure out how you can help the most. While we're waiting, you can tell me what Grewal has on the LaSalle case."

"Have you had lunch?" he asked.

"No, but I'd rather you tell me about the case."

"Okay, maybe we can go for dinner?"

"I'm busy."

"Drinks?" When I glared at him, he smiled back. "Fine. All business it is."

He looked over his shoulder, and then back at me. "No point in asking you to keep it quiet from Grewal, he'll know the information came from me. Here are the highlights. She was looking for proof a serial killer was operating here. Not investigating the killings, but looking for something that would force us to act."

"We know that." At least we knew the serial killer part. The fact she was smart enough not to investigate gave us a new perspective on her; she had some sense.

"Her notes don't tell us if she suspected anyone, but they do list a bunch of murders that might be related. We've eliminated most of them as separate incidents."

"Most?" I knew what was coming even though I hoped I was wrong.

"The two murders you have, Tripton and Sandhu," he said. "We haven't eliminated them."

"Because we're investigating, or because they are part of a pattern?"

"We haven't figured out the pattern yet. Grewal is getting ready to call for a joint briefing. He's trying to figure out how to hang onto his team and take your cases."

If Grewal planned to leave me and Leigh with Mary Copp as our only file, we'd lose any chance of tying them to one killer. "If I can see the files and the work his team has done..."

"Not while Grewal is around," David said.

That sounded like yes. "When? Leigh should be with us," I said. "And Rory, so we have a record."

He held up his hands. "Slow down. We want to keep this quiet, right? So just you and me. How about after dinner? We could go to a nice place, have a glass of wine..."

This guy was persistent, and it wasn't like I found him repugnant. Far from it. He was good looking and charming, and he was giving me what I wanted. And, most importantly, he didn't remind me of Jake.

My phone rang before I answered him. Leigh.

"You need to get out here," she said, adding the location as a medical building on Broadway.

This was important, maybe even case-breaking important.

"On my way." I hung up and grabbed my purse. "Okay, two things. One, go through our findings while I'm gone so you're up to speed. And, don't pass anything on to Paul Grewal until Leigh gives you the go-ahead.

"What about dinner?"

"Sure, but dinner will be pizza here, or in your war room." I didn't wait for him to argue.

Chapter 30

Rory was waiting for me outside the building when I arrived ten minutes later.

"Hurry up, we might be missing something." He grabbed my arm and opened the lobby door.

"Your camera will catch anything that happens," I said, pulling free. "You did leave it running?"

"Yeah." He punched the elevator button for the tenth floor. "This is Mary Copp's psychologist. Her sister told us about her. And she isn't holding to the client confidentially thing."

We got out and Rory led me to an office door halfway down the corridor. "Why?"

"She thinks Mary is the killer, and she has a loophole about reporting a possible crime."

We entered the reception area and the woman behind the counter waved us to the back. There were no patients waiting. Maybe she didn't have a lot of them, or maybe they'd been sent home.

As we walked through to the office, I realized I was

disappointed. I wanted Hargreaves to be the killer. I felt sorry for Mary and couldn't help but see her as a victim.

Leigh introduced me, and I sat in the chair beside her while Rory headed for his camera.

"Dr. Khatri has agreed to give us information on Mary," Leigh said. "It's something we both should hear. Please go ahead."

The doctor, Aahna Khatri according to the certificates on the wall, looked to be in her fifties. She reached for the folder on her desk. "Please call me Aahna, it's easier."

I nodded for her to continue.

"Mary Copp came to me on her own volition." Aahna started what sounded like a practiced speech. "I will save the medical terminology for an official report if needed, but she suffers from a mental disorder. It prevents her from seeing a larger perspective. The disorder manifests in highly focused activities at the detriment to a healthy social and public life."

"Like stamp collecting?" I asked.

Aahna laughed. "Not stamp collecting in general, but this is common in people who the media label as hoarders. The obsession to collect isn't restricted to stacks of papers, or other physical objects. With Mary, it was always objects like coins or maps or...well, anything small, and if she could save it as an image, even better. The disorder causes the focus, the patient determines the object of the obsession, whether consciously or unconsciously."

"So, Mary could be stalking a someone," I said. "How far would she go?"

Aahna pursed her lips and touched the folder again. "Hard to say. If I could talk to Mary, I may be able to find the truth over time. But she is in a coma, and all this is supposition."

"Would you write a report for the files?" Leigh asked. "Would you be willing to testify in court?"

"I will obey whatever official compulsion comes to bear. I would prefer until then that you keep my contribution anonymous. While I believe I am within the law giving you my opinion, it will damage the trust I've built with my clients. A circumstance I would like to avoid if possible."

Leigh wanted me here for some reason, and it wasn't just to witness Dr. Khatri's story. The only reason I could think of on the spot was I would ask questions she couldn't. "Do you think Mary is capable of killing someone? And more than once?"

"I'm able to tell you this information because I feel Mary is, or was, about to harm someone. I cannot say whether Mary would hurt herself, or a stranger. As to killing, we all have it in us to kill, Charity. Thankfully, most of us never reach the point where we trigger the ability."

"Could she be a serial killer?" I asked.

"I will have to give some thought to the question to fully answer you, but for now, I would say no. She doesn't exhibit the characteristics of that particular psychopathy. She has empathy and she cares about her sister. She has difficulty making friends, so perhaps that strengthens my thought she isn't. Serial killers are generally quite charming when they want to be. That is how they lure their victims. Mary was lacking in charm."

I looked at Leigh, but she gave me no clue about what else she needed from me. "If Mary wakes up, would it be advisable to ask her about her attack?"

"I'm sure you've spoken to her doctor," Aahna said. "She may not remember the attack, but perhaps she will remember something to help find her attacker." She touched the file again. "I wouldn't ask her if she was a killer. She should speak with a professional before you interrogate her."

Leigh stood. "Thank you for your time," she said. "We'll try to give you advance notice if this goes public. Here's my card, if you think of any other details we should know."

Aahna took the card and turned it over. "I will call, Detective, but I don't think I will think of anything else."

I followed Leigh out, Rory trailed us with his equipment. In the lobby, I asked Leigh to stop. "Why did you need me there?"

"Do you think she was telling us the truth?"

I closed my eyes to run the meeting through my truth filter. "Yes, and no. I think she was holding something back. And I'm suspicious about how easily she gave us the information. But when we review Rory's recording, I'm pretty sure we got more general stuff about mental illness than we got specific details about Mary."

"Good. That's what I thought more or less. Everything she told us could have come from Mary's sister." Leigh dug her keys out of her purse. "Do you think Mary did it?"

"Possibly, but I don't know." It was hard to get behind the idea that our killer had also been attacked and was in a coma.

Chapter 31

"I need to do this alone," I said after I'd explained what David and I were planning this evening. "I think he'll be more open to suggestion if there are no witnesses."

Rory stood from where he sat across the conference table "Dude? That could be a critical scene."

"Alone," I repeated. "If David agrees, we'll let you set up, but you can't be in the room, and we can't ask for permission since we're sneaking around to do this."

"Fine, but—"

I was running out of time to win this argument. "No buts. Trust me. I might have said no initially, but you've earned the right to be on the team. I'll try to convince him to let you record."

"I'll need to check out the room," he said. "Ten minutes is probably what I need."

"Now that's settled," Leigh said. "What do you mean by open to suggestion? Are you relying on your feminine wiles to make him break the rules?"

"You say that like I don't have any." *I might be rusty, but I wasn't dead.*

"Let me remind you about the restaurant the other night," Leigh said. "Seriously, don't try it with him. David Anchor might not be an asshole, but he's not stupid. He won't let you damage the other case, no matter what you offer."

I hadn't been planning on making him do anything wrong, maybe a bit shady, but not wrong. Why did I feel kind of dirty now?

"I was thinking of something along the lines of getting copies or pictures of documents rather than full on espionage."

"If you copy something, it will leave a record." Leigh crossed her arms and nodded at me to rebut her argument.

"Only if they look for one," I said, proving that I'd thought it through.

"I'm not deleting a recording of a critical scene," Rory said.

And there I was thinking he was on my side. "Don't tell him that if you want to put your camera in the room." I turned back to Leigh. "If we find something that solves even one of the cases, won't all be forgiven?"

"With the brass, yes. But Anchor will start from page one gaining the trust of the other detectives."

I checked the time. David was going to be here with the pizza in a few minutes. "What *can* I do?"

Leigh sighed. "Besides having dinner with a good-looking man who seems attracted to you?"

I thought for a second. "Yes. After the cases are closed." Maybe I was ready to date again.

"Look at it from Grewal's point of view. If you barge in trying to find something to solve our case or looking like you're trying to steal his case, he'll focus on stopping you. But if you go in looking for a way to help him with the LaSalle case, and not take the glory, he might thank you."

"Okay, I'll make sure I get that on the recording." She rolled her eyes. "No, don't worry. I'll be subtle...well, real anyway."

"Do we need more pizza?" Dave said as he stepped into the conference room. He held two large pizza boxes and a six pack of soda.

"Are you expecting a mob?" I asked.

"I like variety, and it's always a good idea to have leftovers for everyone tomorrow, in case we need to smooth some feathers."

Leigh grabbed her bag. "I need to go home. Good luck," she said, glaring at me from behind David's back.

"I gotta set up, then I'm out of here," Rory said. "Val's been missing me. "

"Set up?" David asked.

"My camera. In the other room. I need to film you even if I'm not there."

"Wait." David put down the pizza and soda. "This was supposed to be on the down-low."

"It will only be used if we find something," I said. "Rory doesn't need another boring and unproductive search scene."

He looked at Rory, at Rory's equipment. He looked at me, then the pizza. I guess I should be flattered I wasn't the last thing he considered.

"You can't leave any sign you were in the room," he finally said. "If we don't find anything, I want to see you delete the files."

"Deal," Rory said. "Can I have the keys to the room?"

David shook his head. "I'll take you in and watch you set up."

I picked up the food. "If we're on record, we'll need to keep it professional."

"We won't be in there all night," David said with a smile.

My cheeks heated up; embarrassment or annoyance, I couldn't tell. "I meant the food should stay outside the room," I said.

"Yeah, me too." He laughed.

An hour later he'd finished walking me through the pictures and data on the wall, shown me the list of possible suspects, and summarized the notes they'd gathered.

I let him lead me out to the nearest cubicle. He left the war room door open but didn't want me hanging around inside while we talked. He put the small camera that Rory had given him on the desk, so we wouldn't have blank spaces in the recording.

"So?" he asked, reaching for a soda. The cans were warm now. "Found anything?"

"Why are Jackson Tripton, Alex Sandhu, and Mary Copp on the wall?"

"Grewal listened to your ideas. We haven't uncovered a link, yet. To be honest, we haven't looked. Why?"

"I was hoping it was for a real reason." Something was there, I just couldn't quite grab it. "When did you receive that list of possible victims LaSalle thought the serial killer murdered?"

"It's not complete. We only got it pulled together yesterday." He flipped the lid of the pizza box and let it close without taking a slice. "Your two murders aren't on the list."

"Do you have a list of the methods the serial killer used?"

He stepped into the war room and flicked through a pile of papers. Picking up one of them, he came back. "Stabbing, strangling, one looked like a car accident. The coroner didn't find any indication of murder. One of the people choked to death. Two of them were ODs."

"Don't serial killers stick to one method usually?"

"Yeah and there's usually a ritual, but if LaSalle was right, this one just likes to kill. Or maybe we just can't see a link yet."

"What if there is a connection?" I asked. "Not the killing, but the motive."

He went back into the room. I followed because that 'something' I'd sensed was starting to solidify.

"Nothing here about motives," David said. "If these victims weren't all listed as homicides, we wouldn't be able to guess at why they were targeted."

"Here's the deal," I said. "We have three people we think might be our killer. If there's a link between these cases, maybe looking for connections to our suspects would tie it up."

"You up for an all-nighter?"

That came with a few meanings, but I let it go. "Let me text Rory about the battery life of his cameras."

It took four hours of internet searches and queries of official databases, but we'd managed to link almost all the deaths in some way to Hargreaves, McBain, and with a few wiggles of reality, to Mary.

Chapter 32

It was really early, but I didn't want to wait to talk to Leigh. Rory would have to be happy with a recording of my side of the phone conversation.

She picked up on the fourth ring, just before I went to voicemail, I'm guessing.

"What?" she mumbled.

"Sorry to wake you. I'm at the office, and we found something."

"Let me talk to Anchor." Her voice sharper this time.

"He's gone home," I said. "I kind of tricked him into thinking I left too."

I heard a thump on her side of the call. "Should I join you?"

"I need some sleep, so I'm hoping you decide not to."

"What did you find?" The phone was on speaker now. I hoped she wasn't getting dressed.

"There was a list of what LaSalle thought were victims of the serial killer. David and I did some research and they all link back to our suspects." I was fading fast, so I kept talking so she couldn't slow me down. "I didn't find a clear winner, but we didn't have to work very hard to tie them to Hargreaves. It's the same as you and I found. The problem is that they all connect somehow to her husband. Sometimes because he's her husband, but a few because of his business."

"And Mary Copp?"

"Not nearly as clear," I said. "But yes, using the photos from her shrine, we linked them all to her."

"I guess you were right," she said. "Grewal's case doesn't stand alone. He's going to hate this."

"That's why I need to sleep to be presentable tomorrow," I said. "David is going to set up a meeting. Kardozian will be there. We can explain what we found."

"I suppose you won't let David do all the talking?"

"That would make it look like he was the one to make the connection. We need the glory here." I heard a deep sigh on the other end. "I know it's not a competition, but you can't let anyone think you aren't capable, Leigh." Even I knew that.

"Can you meet me for breakfast?"

"We should be back here by eight," I said.

"David won't start without us. He's not that kind of guy, and he doesn't have enough background to persuade them. We need to get our ideas straight."

"Will you call Rory?"

"Yeah, what about the recording?"

"I'll text him that it's in the cloud as soon as we're finished here."

"Okay, get some rest. We'll meet at the diner?"

"I'll be there."

"Charity, one more thing."

"Yes?"

"Don't spend the next few hours trying to make the facts fit your desire to arrest Hargreaves."

I laughed. "I won't. I'm too tired."

We hung up. I texted Rory on my way out after locking his equipment in our war room.

Chapter 33

I ended up getting almost enough sleep, meaning I was awake enough to make decisions but too tired to worry about them being right. I had heard Leigh's warning, and I told myself I would be careful not to step over the line. This was the best shot we had to link these cases together.

We were in the LaSalle war room. It made sense because they had so much more on display than we had in ours. Rory stood in the corner tending his cameras. He'd set up five of them and used his tablet to control them, at least that's what I thought he was doing.

Over breakfast we'd gone through the details and planned our approach.

Kardozian opened the briefing by encouraging open-mindedness. Now it was my turn.

"We can probably keep this short," I said. "David gave me the opportunity to look at your work on LaSalle. Don't blame him, please. I did make my case and he thought there might be something to it."

"And I figured letting her look would end her nagging." He winked at me.

Was that why he flirted with me? Softening me up so he could stop me from pushing to link the cases? I had to leave the answer for later. This was not a time to bring up personal issues.

"It took a while. You managed to amass a ton of information." That should stroke their egos.

"Obviously not the right information," Grewal said. "David's convinced me you actually found something rather than made assumptions. Just get on with it."

"Paul, let her do it her way," Kardozian said. "If this was your presentation, you'd be showboating."

Grewal grinned in acknowledgment. "Okay, Sarge."

I looked over at Leigh. She nodded to me to continue.

"You had the right information, or at least your part of it. It's like a jigsaw. There is one picture to create. We have the edge pieces and some of the sky, and you have all the little colorful pieces to fit together to make the pretty flowers."

They shifted in their seats and started looking around the walls for hints as to what the hell I was talking about.

"You had the information on LaSalle's search for a serial killer, and you had a list of people she thought were victims. Our three victims were there, but in with a lot of names, so you wouldn't put that together yet. You added another name we were sure was a victim. Helena Tripton, Jackson's sister."

"We didn't miss the connection," Grewal said. "We haven't had time to ask about them."

"I'm not blaming you," I said. "You also didn't know what we found out about the shrine we found in Mary Copp's house." I held up a hand to stop him interrupting my flow. "Mary Copp, who's in a coma on the floor of VGH where LaSalle died."

Grewal looked at the notes one of his detectives was

making. He nodded at what he saw and waved me to continue.

"You also aren't aware we have three suspects on our cases. Three people who might have committed all the crimes, not just a suspect for each."

"I haven't updated you with that, Paul," Kardozian said.

"All those little points gave David and me a new lens to filter your information. We found all but two of your potential victims in one or more photos from the shrine. We think the last two are in a few pictures, but the focus is on Hargreaves, so there's not enough detail."

"We asked the techs to try to clear them up," David said.

"Then we started searching for more connections," I said. "In the end, your victims were all tied in some way to our three suspects, in addition to being in the photos."

Grewal turned to Leigh. "Who are your suspects?"

Leigh pointed him back to me. I could see she was holding in a smile, and I hoped it meant I was handling this right.

"Mary Copp. She had the shrine in a hidden room in her house. Even her sister didn't know about it. The pictures show she had an obsession with Cecilie Hargreaves. The sister says Mary was obsessive about her interests since childhood. Her psychologist hinted it is possible for Mary to escalate to murder. The theory is she's removing people she thinks are blocking her access to Hargreaves."

"We have concerns," Leigh chipped in. "It is a very large leap of coincidence to believe someone wanted to kill Mary Copp who was herself a murderer."

"Possibly revenge from a relative of a victim," Grewal said.

"Since we didn't know about an active killer, I think it unlikely a civilian would find Mary," Leigh said. "But it's a point to consider."

"Also, we think there's a possibility the shrine was staged, even though it was in a hidden room." I handed around a picture of the room as we found it. "Suspect number two is Ernie McBain, Hargreaves' husband."

I waited until they finished looking at the photo before continuing.

"He is closely linked to the victims, and he married Hargreaves pretty fast after her first husband died in suspicious circumstances. He could be the one taking all the pictures, if the shrine was staged."

"Almost all the links to McBain pass through from Hargreaves," David added. "That gives him the same motive as Mary Copp. Also, getting Hargreaves as a client will mean a lot of money if her comeback is successful."

"Our last suspect is Hargreaves. The connections to your victims and ours is the strongest. Directly linked for most, like her husband, her husband's sister. She's acting suspiciously, at least in my mind. Constantly elbowing into the investigation. Getting angry when we ask questions." I shut up before I said she was the killer.

"The problem with her as our suspect is, she's high profile," Leigh said. "It's hard to see how she would be able to kill all these people without someone witnessing."

"Maybe she kills witnesses," I said. "That's the motive, people who could identify her. The guy who called in Mary Copp's attack is dead."

I had no more to add. Or there was no more to add without telling them my theory was right without any clear evidence.

Paul checked the guy taking notes again, then stood. "Okay, so you think the culprit is Hargreaves or the husband. I understand the gut feeling, but the Crown Prosecutor can't win a case based on instinct."

Did all cops run the same script when someone had an idea?

"The best way to figure it out is to make a list of the suspects and begin eliminating them. Not pick a suspect and start proving their guilt." Grewal put a new flip-chart paper over the pictures on his wall.

"But that will take too long," I said. Then realizing how petulant I sounded, I added, "I mean, what if another murder is in the works? McBain might already be poisoned. The witness is dead. Isn't that how serial killers work? They can't stop until we catch them?"

"Most serial killers have a compulsion to kill," Kardozian said. "This person seems to be stuck trying to solve the same problem over and over. They'll stop when the problem goes away."

"Or until we catch them," I said. "And if the killer solves their problem? Do they go free?"

"We don't have much history with that kind of motive," Grewal said.

I think he meant it kindly, but all I saw was a big wall he was building with Leigh and me outside and all the cases inside.

"If we figure out the problem Cecilie Hargreaves is trying to solve, we can catch her." I was on automatic now. No matter how loud the voice in my head yelled I should try to get along, their attitude that the professionals would take over now pressed all my buttons and flicked all my switches.

"And if it's not her, we waste time while a killer keeps going," Grewal said, his voice getting louder.

Kardozian rose and took a step to get between us. "Enough. Leigh, Charity, thank you for the update. I've authorized copies of everything Detective Grewal has to be made available to you. You'll find it in your room." She pointed to the door. "Rory, we don't need you recording here now."

We were dismissed. That got through my anger. Kardozian was taking Grewal's side. Bad enough she'd told us to leave, but Rory wasn't her employee and since *he* didn't argue, I started marshaling my words. Then Leigh touched my arm.

"Charity, let it go." She gave me a tiny push toward the door.

Rory headed our way, equipment bundled in his hands.

"We've got a lot of stuff to go through," Leigh said, herding me to the door.

I gave up. We still had David, the one person in the room who might tell us what happened.

"Anchor, go with them, please."

Kardozian ended my last hope that we weren't cut out.

Chapter 34

"What the fuck?" I exploded as soon as our door shut. "Did they just send the kids from the room?"

Leigh plopped into one of the chairs. "It sure felt like they did."

"Did I do something wrong?" I tried to run the entire meeting in my head like a movie, but it kind of stuck on the last few seconds. "I mean, before the end?"

Leigh opened the door to accept delivery of boxes. Presumably the copies of Grewal's work. "You did fine," she said. "You had me convinced."

Rory started helping her put the boxes on the table.

"Paul won't let go of the work we did," David said, checking the inventory sheet that had come with them. "He'll need convincing and that is what Kardozian is doing right now."

That cooled me off a bit. "You mean the adults were sent out of the room? So, the kids could be lectured?"

He chuckled. "Something like that, but if Paul hears you call him a brat, you'll never get him on-side." He placed the list of contents down. "The files are complete. I'm guessing he's got a copy of your work."

"Another waste of time," I said. I didn't like the idea that someone had gone through and copied all our work.

The boxes were full of written statements and photos. It was going to take hours to sort through. "This would be easier and faster if we worked together. If we didn't have to go through this stuff as separate teams."

"You did that last night," Leigh said. "And with fresh eyes. If we only look at Grewal's wall, we'll see his thought process, not ours."

"How are we going to fit it in?" I looked for blank space on our walls and windows. There was some, and more than Grewal had, but not enough.

"We'll think of something." Leigh followed my gaze. "David, can you squish what we have up a bit? You need to check it all anyway."

He turned to take in the whole content. "Does Rory have this all on record?"

"Yeah, but I'll do it again." Rory moved to the doorway and slowly panned the room. "It would be awesome under the opening credits."

"I think we should start from scratch," David said. "That way we'll all review everything in a new light. It won't take longer to reorganize everything into one."

This mundane conversation had brought me back to my usually partly sunny attitude. David had a point, rebuilding the picture would probably take less time than finding a way to integrate Grewal's stuff.

"The sergeant is on the way," Rory said. He moved around the boxes back to his corner.

The door opened and Kardozian stepped in. "I see you have the case files I ordered for you."

"Thanks for this, Sarge," Leigh said.

"I'm sorry about what happened," I said. I wasn't really sorry, but it was time to hone my getting along skills.

"Tempers get high when cases stall," she said. "If people aren't passionate about the case, I worry."

"So, what happens next?" Leigh asked. "Are we combining forces?"

Kardozian shook her head. "I think keeping your team together is a better approach. I don't want conflict to get in the way of progress. You will parallel Paul's investigation. Your primary focus will still be the three cases we gave you. Paul's will be LaSalle. The change is that you'll share everything. These rooms are to remain unlocked during shift. You'll have keys to both rooms."

The idea Detective Grewal could poke around our investigation made me anxious, until I realized that was exactly the way he must be feeling.

"Paul is losing a detective," Kardozian said. "So, David, I'll ask you to work with both teams, act as a liaison."

"Keep things from erupting?" he asked.

"That would be nice," Kardozian said. "Just make sure information is flowing."

"How does Detective Grewal feel about that?" I asked. "I mean, we're happy to cooperate, but he's kind of territorial."

"Charity, don't push him and he'll be fine. Remember, I was the one who decided you'd keep your investigations separated. That worked. You've found viable suspects. Paul has, too. Now you need to work together."

It sounded like an end-of-discussion statement.

"Who is Paul losing?" David asked.

"Ian Clark," Kardozian said. "We've got another murder."

She left before I got the chance to ask for details.

"Not all murders are connected, Charity," Leigh said.

"You know me too well," I said, laughing. "Let's get this sorting going before I need a nap."

We worked fast, no arguing, no long explanations of why things were linked. Leigh said we could refine it later. Rory set his camera on a stand and took on the role of placing things on the wall. At the end of two hours, we had a solid representation of the cases. We'd isolated our three names and another two from Grewal's case.

"It almost looks complete," I said. "The links are better with this version." We'd decided to create like an organizational chart for each suspect. "I guess I understand why all these people are suspects, but where do we start with eliminating them?"

David was standing beside the chart. "We could each take one of them and work separately."

"There are too many," Leigh said. "We'll take the two new ones, and you take the three we found. Fresh eyes, right?"

The phone rang. Leigh answered it and then put the call on speaker after a moment.

"Please identify yourself." She made a writing motion and I picked up a pen and sheet of paper.

"You'll know me when we meet. I can assure you it is worth your while." The voice could have been a man or a woman, the words raspy and whispery at the same time.

"We need to know what you have to tell us first," Leigh said.

There was no response, but the person was still on the line. I made a note of the background noise, it sounded like a party.

"What I have to tell you will help you find the killer."

"Which killer?" Leigh asked.

"There is only one," the voice said. "Tonight, Lumber-man's Arch. Ten thirty." The line went dead.

Chapter 35

The caller hadn't said 'come alone', but we figured a crowd would scare him or her away. David wasn't happy, but he agreed to keep it between us until after Grewal's team left. Just before we took off, I dropped a note on Grewal's desk with our progress and an invitation to pop by to look at our work. And that we were meeting a potential lead tonight. The rules of the game were met, perhaps the spirit was still hungry.

At ten twenty-five, Leigh pulled her car into the closest spot to Lumberman's Arch and we got out. We weren't crazy, Leigh had her gun. I didn't own one, so I was relying on her to defend us if things went sideways.

A few hours ago, David had found a place to hide and observe the area, and Rory was filming us from his seat in the back of Leigh's car. He'd set up a rig that allowed him to be on the floor with his camera attached to the window. No one should notice it there.

"There's no one here," I said.

Lumberman's Arch is in Stanley Park, kind of behind the aquarium, if you keep walking toward the water. It's always colder here. The arch is really two giant logs standing up and leaning on each other, and one more touching the top of those and the ground. More like Lumberman's triangle.

There were plenty of trees to hide in; useful for us, but also a great place to lurk. Stanley Park Drive runs between the water park and the concession. During the day, lots of people hang around or cruise past. Right now, no cars, no people, just a feeling like we were being watched.

"Did you expect them to be standing in the open waiting for us?" Leigh asked. She approached the concession stand, which was closed behind shutters for the night. "I wish we'd stopped for coffee."

"You won't be here long."

The voice came from beside the stand. No one stepped around and I still couldn't tell if it was a man or woman.

"Come out, and tell us why you brought us here," Leigh said.

"I expected you to come alone," the voice said.

"Then you should have said that. This is my partner. What you want to say to me, you say to her."

I heard a sharp breath like they were going to argue. I leaned toward the side of the building, hoping to catch a glimpse of them. No luck. Someone, probably this person, had taken out the lights.

There was silence long enough to hear an owl shriek from the trees, and the sound of a car engine. We waited until the vehicle had driven past us and out of sight.

"We don't have all night," Leigh said. She started walking to the side of the building.

I realized we had no idea where David was or if he could see us. Rory might be able to pick the sound up with the microphone, but if he was still in the car, we wouldn't be in the shot if we moved.

"Stop," the voice said.

Leigh didn't obey, a few more steps and she'd be in the shadows. "Are you going to tell us why we're here?"

"Leigh," I said.

She turned to me.

The informant, dressed in a black hoodie, black pants, and wearing gloves, stepped behind her, swinging a bat.

"Duck!" I screamed it out, so David would hear.

Leigh moved, and the bat hit her on the right shoulder.

She stumbled and turned. I saw her reaching for her gun with her left hand.

The attacker raised the bat again.

I ran toward them.

The bat came down.

Leigh dodged again, taking the hit on her upper arm on the same side.

I reached them and bowled into the attacker, unbalancing him or her. I managed to knock the bat away as they hit the ground.

A definitely female voice swore.

Leigh was struggling to stand.

I heard footsteps. Hopefully David running to help, and not an accomplice.

The mystery woman got to her feet and glanced around for her weapon.

I took a step toward her.

She ran.

I turned my attention back to Leigh.

"Leave me, go after her." Leigh managed to get to her feet, her arm dangling.

"David can do that," I said. "We need to get you some help."

"Dude," Rory said, running up. "Are you okay?"

"Tell me you got that," I said.

"All of it." He grinned. "It's going to be the trailer. Man, this is great."

"I lost her," David said, rounding the side of the building. "I should have been here."

"So you could have been beaten up, too?" Leigh asked, pain tightening her voice.

"No, you did that just fine," he said. "I could have gone after her."

"Did you see anything that will help?" I asked, leading Leigh to the car.

"Flash of hair," he said. "I got a noseful of some kind of perfume, too."

"Let's talk about it when Leigh's taken care of," I said. He wasn't the only one who smelled perfume.

Chapter 36

I drove us to VGH, not necessarily the closest hospital, but better for traffic than St. Paul's. David followed us, promising to call Kardozian on the way. Leigh just sat silently, bracing her arm against her body.

At the ER, Leigh disappeared behind a curtain and I was sent back to the waiting room until the doctor saw her. I think they wanted to make sure I hadn't beaten her up before they left us together.

˙EXACTLY WHAT HAPPENED?˙ Kardozian strode into the ER behind David almost forty-five minutes later. "How bad is she?"

My mind was going in all kinds of directions, so the two different questions made me pause.

"Check it out," Rory said, handing Kardozian his camera. "The shot is dark, but I can clean that up."

David sat beside me and we waited as Rory showed Kardozian how to fast forward to the important part of the recording. "How are you doing?" he asked.

"Not the first time I've been around that kind of violence," I said. It was the first time I hadn't been the target of the attack. "The adrenaline rush has me a bit shaky, but I'll be fine. You?"

"Pissed. I should have been closer, and I should have caught the runner."

"Detective Anchor, report, please."

David stood and reeled off the facts. "We'd planned for an informant. My job was to observe and track them. It turned out to be a trap. Leigh didn't make any mistakes. I would have done the same as she did."

"Now we have an officer injured, and no information," Kardozian said. The words didn't come across like she was pointing fingers, but I wasn't a great judge of that kind of thing.

"We had no way of knowing," I said. "What should we have done?"

"In hindsight? Taken a lot more back-up." She looked at me as she spoke, and her attitude changed. I don't know what she read on my face, but she added, "Charity, David is correct. Given the information you had at the time, you took the right precautions. Just...just give me a heads up if you're contacted again to meet someone in a dark alley."

"I hope it won't come up," I said.

The doors opened behind me and Leigh walked through. Other than looking pale and wearing a sling, she seemed normal. Kardozian left us to greet Leigh.

"Dislocated shoulder," Leigh said. "They popped it back in. Thank god it's a slow night."

"How much pain?" I asked.

"It's receding." She dug a bottle of pills from her pocket. "They gave me this to take if the pain gets bad."

"Just be happy it wasn't worse," Kardozian said. "What if they'd used a gun, not a bat?"

"I don't like to deal in what ifs, Sarge," Leigh said. "I need to get the details out of my head now, so there's no time for me to forget."

"I can record it," Rory said. "Do you need someone to ask questions, or can you just talk? Do we need a private place? Maybe you can use your badge to get us a room for a little bit." The last was directed to Kardozian.

"I'll have them open up an office," she said, leaving us for the front desk.

"Did the doctor recommend time off?" I dreaded having to walk away from the cases now but couldn't imagine I'd be allowed to hang around if Leigh wasn't there to babysit.

"He left it up to me," Leigh said. "I'll have to be cleared tomorrow, or later today, I guess."

"Do you want time off?" David asked. "I've seen this kind of thing go both ways."

"No," Leigh said. "I can't leave the cases unfinished. And I can't leave you in charge of Charity, you are not strong enough for that."

David grimaced at the thought, all very comedic. I couldn't exactly deny the point.

"When you go in to the doctor, make the appointment as early as you can," he said. "Don't be on the painkillers if you can manage it. Minimize everything about the incident and he'll probably okay you to go back to work."

"I know how to play the game," Leigh said. "Thanks anyway. I haven't taken a pill yet, and the pain is tolerable. I'm pretty sure the doc will ban me from lifting things, maybe for a very very long time."

"Right, we have a room," Kardozian said. "This way."

We followed her around the corner to a sign that read "Restricted Area". She pushed through the door and opened an office just inside. "Rory, set up, and we'll do this interview."

Kardozian started with Leigh. She repeated the facts almost the same way that David had, so I figured it was a procedural code that I would try to parrot. Then she gave her recollection of the attacker.

"The assailant was a woman," she said. "She was wearing multiple layers of clothing to make her look bulkier, but I could tell when she moved...like she was carrying a couple of inches of bulk rather than it being part of her. Perfume, not too much, I only smelled it when I was close. I think she did something to make herself taller. That's all."

"If you think of something later, you know to enter it into the record," Kardozian said. "Okay, David, repeat the verbal report you gave me earlier, and then give your impressions."

This time I listened very closely to the facts, not to check them, but to make sure I said everything in the right way.

"I didn't get near enough, or I thought I didn't until Leigh said you had to be close to smell the perfume. I got a hit of it, so she must have been hiding nearby. I agree about the clothing, as she didn't move like a person with that much weight. Fat or muscle changes the way you maneuver your body. Height? I would say she came up to my nose, so she'd be about five-eight. I didn't notice anything odd about the way she ran, so she couldn't have been much shorter in reality."

When he stopped, I prompted him, not sure if that was kosher, but it was important. "You said you saw hair."

"Oh yeah. When she was running, some got out of the hood. It was too dark to catch the color, but it must have been long."

"Anything more?" Kardozian asked.

"If I remember anything else, I know what to do," David said.

Kardozian looked at Rory. "Did you see anything that's not on the recording?"

"No, I was on the floor of the car, looking at the screen."

She turned to me. "Okay, go ahead."

I rattled off the same facts, and added, "When I hit her, I felt muscle push back, but it was padded. So, I agree on the couple of inches of clothing. I've been thinking while everyone talked, and I think I hit hips, not belly like I expected. So, two inches too tall."

"Anything else?" Kardozian asked, looking at Leigh.

I followed her gaze. Leigh was fading fast, so no embellishments. "I got the perfume too. And Cecilie Hargreaves wears that scent."

"Is it designed just for her?" Kardozian asked.

"We can find out," I said. "That kind of thing will be in some fan magazine. If that's all, I think we should get Leigh to bed."

I knew what the aftermath of an attack could feel like, and sleep was her best way to look good for the doctor in the morning.

"Meet in my office at nine?" Kardozian asked.

"I'll see the doc early," Leigh said.

Rory packed up his equipment. "That's plenty of time for me to work with the footage and clean it up."

"You keep an original copy, right?" Kardozian asked. "We'll need an unaltered version for any charges."

"Duh," Rory said. "I'm a professional."

Chapter 37

The next morning, we had good news. Leigh could stay on the job. No lifting or straining her shoulder for a couple of weeks.

At nine o'clock, Kardozian called us into a new meeting room. This one was large enough for Grewal's team, ours, and a few guests if necessary. A screen on one wall showed that image from an old TV network sign off; a kind of bullseye with pictures around the edge.

Rory joined Kardozian at the front of the room and as soon as we all settled, she started.

"You all have the report on last night's incident involving Detective Andrews." She paused while everyone turned and gave some acknowledgment to Leigh. "Rory MacDonald will take us through the recording, and he'll explain how he processed the video to achieve more clarity." She nodded to Rory and took a seat.

"Let's watch the scene first," Rory said. "Then we'll go through slower and I'll point out the important details."

I glanced Leigh's way. I had only relived my attacks in my nightmares. I wasn't sure how this would hit her, and how much being a cop would ease the emotions. She was sitting rigid, eyes focused on the screen.

The clip was short; everything happened fast. Rory had somehow brought light into the scene, it was grainy but clearer, if that made any sense. The action only took seconds from the moment the bat came out to my knocking her over. Watching it, I realized how close I got to having my head smashed in. Leigh still stared at the screen, lips pale from the pressure of pressing them closed.

Rory stopped the action. "So, from the interviews last night, we were pretty sure the attacker was female, not some guy with a high voice." He rewound and then froze on a shot with the attacker holding the bat high just before she hit Leigh. "I did some research, and the way the bat is held and the way the person is balancing from the hips indicate strongly that this is a female."

"The boobs help too," Paul Grewal called out.

Rory used a laser pointer to show what Paul meant. "I'm not sure when the last time you saw a set of boobs was, Detective, but that's a fold in the layers of clothing."

Everyone chuckled, even Leigh.

When working in his area of expertise, Rory reminded me of his dad. All the fake surfer dude language gone, he stood straighter, dressed slightly more conservatively, and he controlled the room. If he got a chance in the film industry, he was ready to make the most of it.

"What did you do to clear up the shadows?" Another of Grewal's detectives asked.

"I adjusted the levels. It hides a lot of the dark without altering any details."

"Did your research turn up anything else?" Detective Clark asked. He was assigned to the new case, and I made a mental note to find out what that was.

"There are a few flashes of the face where it's

exposed," Rory said. He changed the shot to a collage of pictures: parts of eyes, shapes of noses, a tiny part of an eyebrow. "Is that enough for facial recognition?"

"I sent it off," Kardozian said. "Don't hold your breath. If they find anything, it could take weeks."

If only Hargreaves had a distinctive mark near her eyes, we'd have her.

"All we have is a female suspect and a guess at her height and weight," Grewal said.

"That's more than we had before," Leigh said.

"We have a few things found at the site by the techs," Kardozian said. She reached into a box at her feet. "A footprint cast. That will be helpful if we find the shoes. A few hairs stuck to the siding of the building. Not sure if they belong to our attacker, but Detective Anchor saw long hair and these strands are broken off at forty-five centimeters. And we found this." She held up a bag containing what looked like a toy microphone.

"A voice changer?" David asked. "Prints?"

Kardozian put the bag away. "Yes, and we'll see."

"She was wearing gloves," Grewal said.

"Maybe she picked it up before putting them on," I said.

Leigh nudged me and gave me a glare. Okay, so maybe my tone was less than respectful, but he started it.

"This hasn't been to the lab yet," Kardozian said. "No prints found at the scene, but the lab might pick up some the field equipment can't. We might find DNA. You have to breathe when you use this, so that's more promising."

She put the lid on the box. "Rory, anything else?"

"I'll keep looking," he answered. "The detail isn't great, and if you don't want me to be aggressive with the processing, I can't promise."

"Any more questions?" Kardozian asked.

"Next steps, Sarge?" Grewal asked.

"Keep your investigations going. Take care if you get a call to meet for a tip. Rory will send you stills of the facial shots. Try to eyeball a match to anything you have."

The meeting broke up. Leigh and I waited for Rory while David headed back to start poring over the pictures.

"Dude, that was epic," he said.

"Nice to have you back," I said.

Leigh touched my shoulder. "We need to get out of here for a bit. I can't think in here."

"I'll get David," I said.

"No, just us," she said. "Rory, I'll trust you to be discreet. When I said I can't think, I meant I can't hold myself together much longer."

Being strong for the team had taken a lot out of her. Rory went to the war room for our bags and to think of something to tell David so he wouldn't follow us. Leigh and I headed for the elevator.

"We just need to get in the car," I said. "We'll go to my place."

She held on until we were away from the station. Then a huge gasp for breath signaled the end of her control.

I glanced in the rear-view mirror to check what Rory was doing. There was no camera in sight, and he was looking at the passing traffic.

Within fifteen minutes we were sitting in my living room. Rory had taken the car to park after I stopped in the no-parking zone at the top of my street. He walked in with a tray of lattes and cookies. Leigh had her emotions cooled and was relaxing on the couch.

"No one hears about this," she said, reaching for the coffee.

"Dude, they'd understand." Rory put the cardboard tray in my recycling bin.

"You have no idea," Leigh said. "Yes, they'd all commiserate and share stories of when they'd broken down. Then every time I got even as much as a paper cut, they'd toss me tissues. I don't want to deal with that."

"That's why you didn't want David around?" I leaned against the counter.

"Partly, but I think we need to talk about what happened. We've been on this from day one, so we might realize something that no one else would."

"So, does this mean Mary Copp is off the hook?" Rory asked. "I mean, she's still in a coma, right?"

I'd called the hospital to check this morning. "Yes. And it's hard to imagine that she arranged something like this before she was attacked."

"So, it's for sure Cecilie Hargreaves?" He took a giant bite out of a peanut butter cookie.

"Feels like it," Leigh said. "There are other women on the suspect list. We need to find out about the perfume. And we need to confirm where she was last night. But it could be that she and McBain are working as a team. Or someone else like Mary is out there and using Hargreaves' scent. We just don't have enough."

"What if we let the others work on that theory, and we focus on Hargreaves?" I asked. "I know we're supposed to be eliminating people, but when do we change tactics?"

"We can't hide that from David," Leigh said. "You'll have to bring him on board."

Not a no.

Chapter 38

When we got back to the station, David was finishing his review of the photos.

"Look, maybe I should have reached out right away, but we got a call. They said Charity was the target, not you. Said they weren't stupid enough to plan an attack on a cop."

"Then they should have told me to come to the meeting. And why did they attack Leigh?" I asked. "I don't care if they meant it to be me."

"We can't let a civilian get hurt," David said.

"I'll just keep investigating if you kick me off the team," I said.

"Did you tell the Sarge?" Leigh asked.

David glared at her as if her question was stupid. "Yes."

"What did she say?"

"Just what Charity said." He glanced over Leigh's shoulders at Kardozian's office.

Leigh turned to see what caught his attention. "Shit," she said.

"What? There are people in with her," I said.

"Yeah, that's her boss," David said. "They've been in there a while. I tried to find out why, but no one is talking."

"Did you listen at the door?" I joked. Everything was glass, nowhere to hide.

"I called a few people I know to ask if they had any idea why the brass was visiting. I hoped it was just the heat on Grewal's case, but no luck."

I hustled them into our war room, where Rory was already set up and waiting. "We have a plan," I said.

"Not a plan," Leigh said. "An idea."

"And not exactly regulation, right?" David said. "You think I won't agree, and maybe run to Grewal? That's why you took off?"

"Yes and no," I said. "I know we haven't completely eliminated the husband, but we're sure Mary Copp is innocent, right?"

"Unless she has a partner," David said. "Maybe the sister?"

"No," Leigh said. She glanced over her shoulder as if trying to see what was going on in the office. The angle didn't work for someone protecting their arm. "Lila is too tall to be the attacker."

"Okay, so what's the idea?"

"Instead of trying to eliminate people, we go after one of our suspects and try to prove it was them." I kept my eyes on his, willing him to agree.

"By one of them, you mean Hargreaves, right?" David put his hand on a pile of pictures beside him.

"It makes sense to me," Leigh said. "If we try to prove it's her, and she's innocent, everything we do could lead us to him."

"These are the photos I inspected. It won't stand up in

court," David said, pushing the stack our way, "but I think it was her last night."

Was he agreeing? I couldn't believe there wouldn't be a debate. "Tell us why," I said as I turned over the top picture. He'd circled the area around her eyes. The next shot was marked in a similar fashion.

"Her eyebrow looks right," he said. "Her nose is the same shape when I found a good shot of it. The problem for the Crown is that there's nothing distinctive. It could be any number of noses, or eyebrows."

Kardozian opened the door and leaned in. Her cheeks were flushed, and she held herself stiffly. "I presume you saw my visitors," she said. stepping in to join us. "The brass takes attacks on our detectives very seriously. Apparently too seriously to leave them in our hands. You'll send copies of all the information that could relate to the attack to Sergeant Vincent. His team will investigate. You will contain your inquiries to the three cases assigned. I've already told Paul the same."

"Not as bad as I thought," Leigh said. "If the attacker is the same person as the killer, do we have to let Vincent's team do the arrest?"

"No, I'm not handing him the closing stats." She sat beside Leigh. "One more thing."

"Fuck." Leigh pushed herself away from the table. "I'm going home, right?"

"Just until we catch them," Kardozian said. "They've convinced Doctor Harrison you'll be involved in more than light desk work. I couldn't change their minds other than to get them to agree that when we bring a suspect into custody, you can come back."

"When does it start?" I asked. She'd go crazy sitting the investigation out. I wasn't planning on leaving her in the dark and I knew better than to ask for permission to keep her in the loop. Without Leigh, it was going to be harder to prove Hargreaves was the killer. David might not be totally on board with my theory.

"You need to pack up and go now," Kardozian said. "David will stay. We can't let Charity run around unsupervised." She tried to add a laugh to lighten the mood, but it just sounded strained.

When she left, I signaled Rory to shut down. He scowled but did as I asked. "We'll update you," I said to Leigh. "Right, David? I'll call and visit with progress reports and to get your input."

Even though I hadn't waited for him to agree, David said, "No way I'm letting the brass cut you out. We all know that the attacker and the killer are related."

Leigh grabbed her bag. "Don't get in shit with Kardozian just to keep me on the case."

"I'll drive you home," I said.

"I'll call a cab," Leigh said. "You both need to figure out how to start proving your theory."

Chapter 39

My odd sleeping times had finally caught up to me. It felt like a case of jet-lag. My mind thought it was afternoon and my clock read two a.m. There was only one thing to do: get some work done so my body might catch up. Okay, maybe not the only choice, but I wanted to work.

I hadn't found a way around the rule of leaving everything at the station. The couple of times I'd tried to log in on my laptop turned out to be a waste of time because I couldn't find a way around the restrictions to what I wanted. So, I brushed my teeth, pulled on jeans, a tee shirt, and runners, and headed back in.

When I got there, I found Ian Clark, the detective in charge of the new murder, bent over the workspace in his cubicle, swearing quietly.

"You can yell if you want, Ian," I said.

"Not a good habit to get into." He looked up at me. "Got a new lead?"

"Just going over the same stuff, hoping for a new result." It sounded too much like the definition of madness.

"How's Leigh?" He picked up a coffee mug and looked inside. "You want me to make a pot?"

I shook my head. The coffee at the station made me long for tea. "She'll be fine. Mostly pissed at being sidelined."

"Yeah, I get that."

"How's the case?" I asked, walking over to join him.

"OD turned murder," he said. "Medical examiner found evidence someone injected the opioids for the victim. No sign of long-term usage, possibly no previous usage."

"Is it Waters?"

"No." He made a note of the name. "Why?"

"Just sounded familiar. Any leads?" I was stalling, and his case interested me; so, it seemed like any case was inter-esting to me, except the ones I was assigned. It also bugged me that people didn't share information. We'd all benefit from more knowledge.

"That's what I'm looking for," he said. "Background on the victim is a bit thin. No record, so no known associates. Family lives in London, the England one, not Ontario. Works from home as a social media marketer."

"Sounds like he chose isolation," I said. "Who found him?"

"Girlfriend. He did have some social life. I guess he wouldn't get jobs if his social media wasn't interesting."

"Is she a suspect?"

"She was in New York when it happened. I haven't had a chance to interview her. She's sedated, apparently freaked out. Doctor said tomorrow." He checked the time. "I mean today."

"Who's working with you?" I wondered if we could fit in some help for him, not that I felt generous, I just wanted in.

"I hoped you'd let Anchor come with me for the interview."

I guess it was inevitable he'd think of David instead of me. A little unsupervised time would be a bonus. "Ian, he's the boss, not me."

Ian yawned. "I guess I should go get some sleep. Hard to interrogate someone when you nod off."

Ten minutes later I was alone. The cleaners hadn't been in yet, so I would be able to look at whatever I wanted. Paul Grewal's investigation topped the list. If only to see if he was being open, or like me only living up to the letter of Kardozian's order. The keys were in one of the evidence boxes in our room. When I finished poking around in his case, I'd see what David might have found in the photos.

The light on the phone blinked. We had a message. I grabbed the keys, paused, reached for the headset, and then stopped. Whatever it was, I could check later. Right now was my best chance to snoop in Grewal's war room.

Inside, I saw how David had managed our process to mimic Grewal's. His walls looked almost identical to the way we'd reorganized ours. I suppressed a childish urge to mix his stuff up and walked the wall.

I noticed some subtle differences in the way he'd placed the photos. We had different suspects, but the links were still marked with lines, only the direction differed. On his, the links came from Hargreaves to the others, rather than the other way around, giving me a new angle. I gave Kardozian silent kudos for knowing her job.

Vancouver isn't a big murder town. Most deaths from crime here came in the form of drug overdoses, gang violence, and the occasional fatal traffic accident. At least that was my take on it from news reports. The cops probably had real statistics. But if I was right, we should have learned about these connections much sooner.

Nothing came at me from my review of Grewal's stuff, so I headed back to our room with an idea. If I took all the pictures David used to try to link Hargreaves to the snippets of images from Rory's recording and cut them so they matched the size and shape of Rory's stills, maybe it would be more clear.

The message light caught my attention as soon as I stepped into the room. I punched in the code to hear the call and put the phone on speaker so I could move around.

"Detective?" It was Ernie McBain. "Oh, a message. Yes. I'm calling because I suspect Cecilie has done something she shouldn't. I don't know what, but she's been very agitated about Jackson's murder and...well, she can be capable of quite dark things. I don't mean murder...no, of course I don't." The pause lasted long enough for me to wonder if the message had been cut off. Then he started speaking again. "Please don't tell her I called. And perhaps I'm overreacting. But now I don't know how to erase this. Please just ignore me. I've had a few too many tequilas."

Chapter 40

I stared at the phone, like it would give up something more. This couldn't be real, it couldn't be that easy. Why would he call rather than come in? Was he setting her up?

I reached for my cell. Too late to call Leigh. No matter what we promised about keeping her updated, she needed rest. Calling David made more sense, a cop would know the next steps. But the last time we responded to a call we'd lost control of the case. And Leigh had been attacked, yes. It could as easily have been McBain calling that time.

If this was a setup, he should be luring me somewhere so he could stop me from continuing the investigation. But he hadn't asked me to go anywhere.

I couldn't make this decision alone. I was too tired to think straight and at the same time, alert enough to lose confidence in my ability to assess risks because I just realized I hadn't even considered calling McBain back. I had one useful idea; call Rory to record this for his documentary.

After I convinced Val to let me speak to him without telling her what it was about, I gave Rory the highlights.

"I'm on my way," he said. "Oh, Val wants to talk to you again."

"Charity, if you get my boyfriend hurt or in trouble, I'll make sure you pay," Val said, then she disconnected.

I hoped she knew better than to come in with Rory. On second thought, it wasn't likely she'd come. Her past experiences with the police made her allergic to their environment.

While I waited for Rory, I called McBain.

He answered on the first ring. "Officer?"

"Charity Deacon," I said. "Do you need assistance?"

"You mean my call earlier? No. I'm afraid the tequila did the talking."

I tried to believe him, but his explanation was so weak. "I need to speak to your wife."

"She's not here. I asked you not to tell her. She's worried about my drinking."

I couldn't force him to take help, but I could apply some official pressure. "You need to come into the station and make a report," I said, hoping it was a real rule. "The message will be in the case file already. You need to deny your allegations for the record."

He sighed in resignation. "I suppose that it's a good thing you won't give her updates," he said. The call ended before I could say anything more.

I was still alone, so I photocopied the pictures David had set aside and started ripping them to match Rory's stills. It was fairly mindless work, so I also thought about how to report this to Kardozian and David after the fact. I couldn't find the words. Perhaps later.

Rory took twenty minutes to arrive. By then I'd taped my versions to the matching ones Rory made, then laid them out like a collage. To my eye the similarities were unarguable. Cecilie Hargreaves attacked Leigh. We just had to find out if she acted alone. If she did, it would tell us whether McBain was a conspirator or a potential victim.

"Okay, dude," Rory said as he entered, "give me a minute to set the shot and then replay the message. Then you can tell me why you called me rather than one of the cops."

I hoped that meant he would still be open-minded about my rationale.

The message didn't contain any more insight the second time. No noise in the background signaling his location, no muffled voice giving him instruction.

Rory turned his camera to include me in the shot. "Do you think this will close the case?"

I looked at the camera to answer, knowing it would seem like I was talking directly to the viewer in the documentary. "This is certainly a big step." I looked down at the collage and decided it wasn't a good time to introduce the visual. "We have a number of questions for Mr. McBain, and Ms. Hargreaves. I am concerned about Mr. McBain's motives for the call. He denied his suspicions when I called back."

I let Rory conduct a mini interview for the film, making sure I got all my theories on the table.

"So where do you go from here?" he asked.

I needed an answer that wouldn't dump me in a vat of trouble as soon as the authorities found out what I said. I'd come to enjoy working with Leigh and didn't want to risk losing the opportunity for the future. "I'll talk to the other detectives, and Sergeant Kardozian for guidance. I imagine we'll bring both Mr. McBain and Ms. Hargreaves in for questioning."

Rory turned off the camera and mic. "Okay, dude, what's the real plan?"

"Leigh needs her rest," I said.

"You don't need to justify your craziness to me," he said. "You called me. I'm guessing it's just us, right? No call to the cops involved."

"You know me too well."

"Actually, Val guessed that. So, like I asked, what's the plan?"

Calling it a plan was generous. "I want to talk to McBain now. Or at least before anyone else gets to him."

"Dangerous," Rory said. "Am I coming?"

"I wouldn't cut you out of the climax," I said. "What do you think will happen if I call David and Kardozian?"

"What will you tell them?"

"My gut says Hargreaves is our killer and McBain has put everything together. And he's done something to piss her off. He's afraid of her and wants that on the record."

"I've seen enough around here to know what the response would be," he said. "Maybe David would go along with you. He likes you. But Kardozian? She'll want everyone protected. She'll need authorization to bring them in."

"We don't have time for that," I said. "If I'm even partly right, he could be dead soon." I remembered how sick he looked a few days ago.

"He left the message when he was sure you were all gone," Rory said. "You've got time."

"I don't think they'll agree with what I want to do," I said as the plan formed in my mind. "I want to make her think she's safe and push her into some kind of confession. You'll record it all on video and we solve all the cases."

"You think you can do that in one day?"

"I don't think we can keep this a secret any longer than that." I wasn't stupid enough to erase the message to buy time.

"Risky," Rory said.

"I get why the cops won't believe me, but do you?" If Rory wasn't on my side in this, I would rethink the whole thing.

"Dude," he said, "I believe you. You always figure it out. Just...well, can we make this work without you ending up in the hospital — or me?"

"Let's get out of here," I said. "We need to find a place where no one will walk in on us."

"Calhoun's?" Rory asked. "I'm starving."

There were a few all-night places in Vancouver, but some of them were less than conducive to private conversations. Calhoun's was one of the best and was far enough away that we wouldn't run into any of the cops I was avoiding.

"Did you drive?" I asked.

"Val dropped me off. It gave her time to hound me about why you wanted to see me. Like she didn't hear the whole conversation, right?"

"Good thing I drove," I said.

Chapter 41

At that time of night, we only took fifteen minutes to drive to the restaurant and find parking on the street. We wouldn't be here by the time rush hour restrictions took effect.

We grabbed our food and sat at a table away from the few students huddled over textbooks.

"Okay, how do we do this?"

"You aren't going to try to convince me to bring David in?" I half wanted him to do that.

"Let me hear the plan," he said. "Hey, I should get this on video."

"No. What if it all goes wrong? You can't deny anything if it's on video."

"I'll delete the file, no problem." He set up the camera, pointed the lens at me, and adjusted something that I assume tightened the focus. That way he wouldn't have to ask people to sign waivers if they were in the shot. "Okay, Charity. If you are going solo on this one, what exactly is the plan?"

He was going to treat this like an interview, which was smart.

"We need to find a way to get Hargreaves off balance. Maybe surprise her somewhere. Then I apply a little pressure and annoy her until she's mad enough to make a mistake." The plan sounded weak, even in my ears.

"What about the husband? Do you still think he's a possibility for the killer?"

"Yeah, it would be good if we got both of them together. I could play them off each other, maybe see if McBain acts like a victim or a perpetrator."

"You haven't thought this through enough," Rory said, his interviewer voice fading into the concerned friend version. "You could use some back-up."

"We need to act fast," I said. "Something made Ernie McBain call us. Even if it is a trap, it means something is coming to a head. I'm worried that someone will die while we wait for approval."

He turned off the camera. "That's probably not enough to avoid an ass chewing, but maybe the sergeant won't toss you in a cell." He finished his muffin. "I probably shouldn't tell Val what we're planning."

"You should tell her," I said. "Don't ever lie to her for any reason."

"I know, I'm not going into details, but we could get her to call the cops if we don't check in. Like an insurance policy."

"If she doesn't lock you up to keep you safe."

"No way. She wouldn't let me do that to her when she was accused of murder. I won't let her stop me getting the best material. Maybe the documentary will turn out to be about you, and not about how the cops do things."

"Maybe they will veto the entire recording if they are worried about image," I said.

"I think you should call David," Rory said. "He's not a bad guy. You need someone to arrest whoever it turns out to be."

"He'll stop us," I said.

"You should try. If you cut him out now, there's no way you'll get together. He likes you, you like him. Why ruin the possibilities?"

"If you're planning to start a matchmaking business, you need to brush up on your subtlety."

"Subtle doesn't work with you," he said. "Hargreaves is recording again, right? Some kind of comeback thing?"

"Yes. She's not going to get far when she's in prison."

"Well, maybe we can spring the trap when she's in a session. Embarrass her in front of the other musicians, yeah?"

"McBain is likely to be there too, right?"

"I have some friends in that business, I can try to find out when and where."

"Do that. With any luck it will be later today," I said.

"Call David before we go too far," he said.

"Or you won't help?" I would do this alone if I had to.

"I'll help, but we need him."

"I'll think about it," I said. "We both need some sleep. Let's get you home."

Chapter 42

At the station early the same morning, Rory and I were waiting for David to arrive. Rory had something, but I knew if I let him tell me now, I'd want to act on it. There'd been no report of any other murders, so despite McBain's call, we still had some leeway.

"Morning," David said. He walked in with a smile, a tray of coffee, and a bag of treats. "Leigh sounded good when I called her."

"Yeah," I said, taking a cup. "We need to talk."

"Am I about to be persuaded to break the law?"

He was only half joking and I wondered what the hell I'd done to earn a reputation for flaunting the law; I didn't have to dig too deep into my memories to find the answer.

"Not as far as I know," I said. There were always some archaic laws still lingering unenforced. "Bend the rules? Are you interested?"

"If I say no," he asked, "you'll do whatever you're planning anyway, right?"

"Yes." No point in pretending. "I want you a part of

this, but I don't think we can risk a major police operation. It will take too long."

"Okay, tell me what you have. If it isn't too crazy, I'm in. If it is, I'm going straight to Kardozian and telling her."

I looked at Rory, but he was no help. I was the only one committed to doing this without the cops. David defended us before. Leigh trusted him. And if Rory was right, he was attracted to me.

"I found a message when I came in last night," I said. Then I proceeded to tell him everything we'd worked out from that point on. What had sounded logical with Rory in the wee hours sounded a little weak when I faced someone with investigative experience. To his credit, David didn't interrupt.

"Is the message still there?" he asked when I finished.

I hit the button and played it for him.

"I'll send a copy to the tech team," he said. "It will eventually make it to the Sarge's desk, but we'll have a day, more or less." He sent a text and then looked at Rory. "So, you did some research?"

"I got something great," Rory said. "McBain is working with a new client. He's spending a lot of time with her. He used to watch Cecilie when she had a session. Now he's blowing her off when she wants him to be with her."

"So, if Hargreaves is the killer, she'll want this girl dead," David said.

"And if it's McBain," I added, "he'll want his wife out of the way. Setting her up for the murders and the attack on Leigh is a good way to accomplish it."

"So, what's the plan?" David asked.

"There's more, dude," Rory said. "Tonight, McBain is in a recording session with the new talent. My friend is working the gig. He said McBain is always with her. We could set him up, record his confession and be done."

"If it is him," I said. "But that doesn't give us Hargreaves."

"Unless we call her to meet us there," David said. "If she sees him paying attention to another singer, it might set her off."

I gave the door a gentle push to make sure it was closed. If we were overheard at this stage, Kardozian might take the case away from me.

"What about Leigh?" I asked. "As her friend, I want her to know what's going on, and I think she'll keep it quiet, but I can't be sure about the detective side of her."

David was digging for something on the table. "I think we keep her out of it," he said. "I've got some brownie points to burn, but she's new. We can tell her when it's done, before we bring in the sergeant." He pulled out a sheet of blank paper.

"I'll trust you to manage the politics," I said.

"It's a first step," he said, grinning back.

"What about the documentary?" Rory asked. "The camera's been on, can I keep it running? I'll need some time to set up wherever we're doing this."

I could tell David was going to shut Rory down. I hoped it was just a cop knee-jerk reaction. "Leave the camera running," I said before he had a chance to answer. "We'll figure out what you need to do with the recording when we're done. Don't show anything to Kardozian before we see it."

"My career is on the line here," David said.

I glared at him. "And Rory has permission to record."

"Fine," he said, holding his hands up in surrender. "If I get fired, maybe you'll have a job for me."

We laughed, but I wondered if he was serious. "Okay, so here's the plan as far as I've thought it out," I said.

David picked up a pen and drew a vertical line down the center of his paper.

"We set up in the studio ahead of time. I think we should try to stay hidden, but I'm not sure how that will work."

"You have a reason to be there for McBain," David reminded me. He made a note on the left side of the line.

"Okay, we'll fine tune that later. We'll arrange for Hargreaves to drop in as a surprise. If she doesn't freak out right away, I'll go in and poke a bit at them."

David wrote more on the sheet.

"They'll confess or accuse. David will arrest the right one and then it's all over except for confirming the list of victims."

"Well, in an ideal world, the plan sounds fine," David said. "Here's what will happen. You need permission from the people who will be in the shot to record."

"I have waivers," Rory said. "And that's our cover, right? We're doing a documentary."

"You might not get permission."

David made a note.

"I can pixelate the image," Rory said. "Don't worry, we'll get permission and I'll record."

"Okay, let's say you're right. The next problem is entrapment." He wrote that down on the left side. "We have to be very careful about what we do to poke them a little. The defense attorney will get everything kicked out if there's a sniff of it."

"Like what?" I wanted this to work, so it was important to know this stuff. Leigh had drummed that into my head enough. "I understand that I can't ask if they killed anyone like I was trying to make them to do it for me, but where's the line?"

"We'll get back to that." David glanced over my shoulder.

I turned and saw the floor starting to fill up with other detectives.

"How are you going to explain why we're there?" David continued. "To anyone, really. I see how Rory might be able to get permission, but why a cop and a PI? And won't Hargreaves wonder? And McBain?"

This planning thing was exhausting. "First, the documentary is about the cops," I said. "We'll say we need some background shots on the people involved. You came because a cop has to be present for the entire shoot."

"And you?"

"She could be your girlfriend," Rory said. "Like at the beginning. The two suspects won't fall for it, but the people at the studio would, probably."

I glared at him, but the look didn't have the same effect as it had on David.

"Might be a problem," David said.

"You don't think I can pretend to be your girlfriend?"

"I didn't mean that," David said. "I'm sure you could be my girlfriend. I mean unless something changes in our relationship, we'd be lying." There was hope in his voice.

I wasn't going to let that get in the way. "I'm still the consultant."

"So that just leaves entrapment." David circled the words on his list of pros and cons. "That's a tricky part. You won't like what I'm going to suggest."

"We'll see," I said.

"We need more people on this," he said. "We need the sergeant to advise us. We need to be able to show this was a legitimate operation."

"No." I was not going to let this get dragged down by bureaucracy.

"She won't shut us down, I promise," David said. "Your plan is actually very good. But we can't do it alone. Remember what happened the last time we tried?"

"But she'll put it in Paul Grewal's hands," I said. "He's senior and he has more detectives on his team. We only have you."

"Thanks for the vote of confidence."

"I meant numbers, not competence and you know it," I said. "What would Kardozian do? Convince me."

He leaned toward me, still smiling, but something had changed. His professional authority overriding the flirting and teasing. "I don't need to convince you. We're the cops and you're a consultant."

His tone carried no threat, and I couldn't tell if he was showing me how Kardozian would react or warning me not to cross a hard line.

"True," I said carefully. "Look, I don't mean to be obstructive, David. I just...this is our case and I'm afraid if we talk about this it won't be. And that's not fair to Leigh."

He leaned back and smiled again. "Perfect. Anyone who tries to push you aside gets that answer. This is our case."

"So, why are we telling the boss?"

"Things will go better if we bug the studio so there's no risk of technical breakdowns. We can get a court order that will make the owners cooperate." He looked over my shoulder again. "We don't need to use the court order unless we run into a block. We also need to consider the safety of the civilians in the room. Kardozian will make sure that happens."

I'm not stupid; stubborn, yes, but I could see the value. "Then we go now," I said. "She's in, right?"

Chapter 43

Kardozian surprised me. She listened and didn't say no, or not exactly.

"David has to be in on everything," she said. "No running off on your own agenda, Charity. You too, Rory. This is a serious operation."

"We'll stick together," I promised. "We'll be in a small room, no opportunity to go maverick."

She looked at me like she'd just bitten a lemon.

"Joking," I said. "David is the boss tonight. We don't jeopardize the cases."

Kardozian rested her arms on the desktop and leaned forward. "You don't know which of them is the killer. That makes it very dangerous. I agree everything is pointing to it being one of them, but if you focus on the wrong one, the best that can happen is they'll get away. The worst? You might end up the next victim."

"We'll pick a suspect each," I said. "That way we can't be surprised." I imagined David standing beside McBain and me facing off with Hargreaves.

"We'll need back-up," David said. "Nearby, not there with us, too suspicious."

"Grewal and his team will be within minutes of your location. They'll be armed, you won't."

Unarmed was fine with me. I had no use for guns in a small spot if tempers were raging. "Okay."

"We don't want anyone hurt," Kardozian said.

Not even a little? I didn't say the words.

"Rory, can you find a way to transmit to Grewal's team?" Kardozian asked. "I don't want to send one of you in with a wire."

"Do you think they'll search us?" I asked. This wasn't the mafia.

"No, but with all the sound equipment, a wire might not be able to transmit." She waited for Rory to answer the question.

"Yeah, I can find a way to do that," Rory said. "Do we need a safe word?"

"It's called a signal word," Kardozian said. "Safe words are for something else. Yes, if you get into trouble and need us to come running, use a phrase."

"Any of us?" I asked. If we needed help, I didn't want to have to worry about the right person being conscious.

"Yes, any of you. We'll use Leigh's name. Any form except just her first. If she comes up in conversation, always Leigh. If you need us to come in fast, Leigh Andrews, or Detective Andrews."

It was a good idea. It probably wouldn't be too weird for us to talk about Leigh during the situation.

"I think we only need the entrapment lecture and we can start," David said. It sounded like standard procedure rather than just for me when he said it.

"In this case, you aren't trying to trick them into committing a crime, simply confessing to one," Kardozian said. "Be careful what you say to start them fighting, or it could look like you are inciting assault — or the defense could make it seem like you are. But I think you're safe."

"I'll keep that in mind," I said. "We should get going to set this up." I stood.

"Wait," Kardozian said. "You can do your set up, but I need you back here before you go in. You need to brief Paul on the fine details, and you need to tell me if anything material has changed."

"And give you a chance to call it off," I said. I tried not to sound bitter, but I still didn't trust that we were going to be allowed to do this. If the plan went right, the case would be over by the end of the day. I would be back doing my own thing soon. Whatever that turned out to be.

"Yes, but I want this to work," Kardozian said. "Does Andrews know about this?"

"I was going to call her as soon as we got out of your office," I said.

"I'll do that," Kardozian said. "I'll try to get her here for the briefing, too. She can't be in the action, but she shouldn't have to miss the results of your work."

"I'll make sure it goes as smoothly as possible," David said. "Thanks, Sarge. For not shutting us down."

"I'm always ready for a good plan, David. Now go catch a killer."

Chapter 44

The recording studio looked exactly like I expected. A small room insulated so much that you could feel the words die as you spoke them. Microphones of all descriptions standing, hanging, and laying around. Separate entrances for the performance space and the sound booth. And one door from the booth to the performance space. Given what we planned, I wanted to be sure of all exits in case things got out of control.

The glassed-in sound booth with its banks of equipment was our home. It was tight, but Rory didn't need to hold any of his cameras. Three of them watched down on the studio from discreet positions, and one in our room from the top of the door.

Rory handed us headphones. "These will be easier than the wired ones they have," he said.

I knew from our plans that these would also transmit to the team waiting for us to call them to our rescue — not part of my plan. I was closing this case unless it killed me. If that happened, David could share the glory with Leigh.

"You sure McBain is okay with this?" Luke asked. He

was the friend Rory called to get us in the door. "I know Jenny said okay. She's happy for the publicity, but if McBain comes in and says no, you'll have to go."

Shit. I assumed everyone would be fine with being on camera if they got to veto the final product. Not that they would get a chance, Rory had two versions of the waiver. Basically, the cops had the only official veto, and friends who would make his life miserable if he didn't listen, aka me. Anyone else who objected got to ask to be pixilated out.

"Mr. McBain has already agreed to being filmed for the documentary," David said. "I'm sure Freyja will enjoy the publicity, too."

I hoped the new singer, Freyja, would follow McBain's lead.

"Okay, they'll be here in a few minutes. Go do whatever you need to so you can stay in this room for a few hours. No one leaves while we're recording," Luke said.

"Is that standard?" I asked. I wasn't planning to hide in here and miss the opportunity to provoke Hargreaves.

"McBain's rules." Luke pulled on his headphones, turned some dials, and flicked some switches.

Rory, David, and I headed for the corridor, David keeping an eye on the street.

"I'm going in the studio if I have to," I said. "David, you'll need to make that happen."

"As long as there's no danger. If someone pulls out a weapon, you are not moving," he said. "Agreed?"

Unlikely anyone would do that, maybe pick up a mic stand, but my training with dodging attacks should be enough to keep me safe. "Agreed, but only if it's a knife or a gun, right? No fair deciding everything is a weapon."

He looked at me, eyes narrowed. "Everything *is* a

weapon. Let's say if I think you'll get hurt, I won't help you leave the room."

I accepted defeat. "Fine. Now anyone need to go to the bathroom?"

"Dude, I'm okay," Rory said. "We don't have much time. If you need to pee, go."

I wasn't going to risk getting shut out.

"Back in the booth," David said. "McBain just got out of a limo and he's helping a girl out."

We hustled back into the equipment room.

"Mr. McBain," Luke said. "And this must be Freyja. I've heard a lot about you."

The girl was maybe eighteen, pale, tall, skinny and had almost translucent blond hair. She smiled and looked to McBain for permission to speak, or maybe it was a look that said, 'see, I'm going to be a star'.

"Thank you, that's so kind of you to say. May I go into the room and make some adjustments?"

"Of course," Luke said.

McBain looked at me. "Why are you here?"

It was like he hadn't called to ask us to help him.

"Getting some background for the documentary." I nodded toward the door Freyja had disappeared behind. "Does she know about it?"

"No. I have power of attorney," he said.

It didn't sound exactly normal procedure. If McBain turned out not to be our killer, I guessed we'd be hearing stories about how poor little Freyja had been taken advantage of by her manager in about five years.

"We'll be with Luke," I said. "You won't even know we're here."

"Fine," he said. "Perhaps I'll make an arrangement with the filmmaker for some footage to use in a video."

"Mr. McBain," David said. "After the session, I'd like to talk to you about the phone call you made."

McBain flushed. "I was drunk, Detective. Please ignore it."

"I'm afraid I can't do that, sir. You didn't come in to make a statement as requested. It will only take a few minutes."

He sighed. "Fine, after. Please don't upset Freyja." He left us to join his budding star.

"He didn't ask about Leigh," I said.

"It doesn't mean he knows what happened to her," David said. "It could simply mean he's an asshole."

"Well, he is that," I said and followed David back into our den.

The singer was good, I guess. I'm not a big fan of pop music these days. She had a husky quality to her voice and her songs weren't all about begging some man to come back to her.

Freyja listened to the guidance McBain gave her over the speaker. Her smile when she heard his voice was a bit too warm to be just a client-manager relationship. It creeped me out. The idea that McBain, in his late forties, if I was feeling generous, and Freyja were involved, would be useful for when Hargreaves arrived.

And she did. At the absolute perfect time. McBain left our booth to stand very close to Freyja, reaching across to adjust her headphones.

Hargreaves opened the door to the booth, stared at the three of us in the corner, didn't say anything, sat in the chair McBain had recently left, and pressed a button. "Hi, sweetie, I came to see your new little project."

McBain swiveled and, for a second, I saw fury in his face. Then he smiled. "Great, I'll be there in a moment. I'd love to get your take on Freyja."

Freyja pouted like she didn't care for anyone's take on her but was smart enough to keep silent.

Chapter 45

My original plan was to head into the recording part of the room and make myself a problem, but here, in the tiny booth, I figured it would be so much easier to get them fighting.

McBain took his time, whispered something to Freyja, finished his adjustments to the headphones and mic, then headed back to us.

Freyja put everything back the way it was by the time he entered the booth.

"Cecilie. I thought you were busy," McBain said. "I would have invited you down."

"I wanted to surprise you." Hargreaves turned her cheek, so he could kiss it.

McBain gave her a peck and turned back to look at Freyja. "Luke, are you ready?"

Luke leaned across and spoke into the microphone. "Okay, Freyja, let's try the opening."

Freyja nodded and stretched her arms, displaying her breasts for Hargreaves. The move meant, 'look at me, I'm young and firm and that's what your husband wants'.

Then she touched her right headphone and started singing.

Hargreaves sat back in the chair. I think she was going for the concentration expression, but there was a little too much sourness around her eyes and mouth.

"Lovely," Luke said a few seconds later when she finished. "Let's take a break."

He got up and left us in the room. Freya wandered out to the hall but didn't come join us.

"She's very green," Hargreaves said. "Young, an asset in our business, but there's no depth to her voice."

That wasn't what I'd heard, but then I wasn't in the business, and I wasn't trying to make her look bad so my husband would dump her.

"Well, she's not you," McBain said. "But I think she's got a good career ahead. She'll have a few hits, we'll send her on a concert tour, maybe she'll be as big as Gaga if I can find her personality hook."

"I hate to argue that, Ernie," Hargreaves said. "You may be right, but she needs a lot of attention."

McBain didn't answer. I guess he knew better than to start a fight in front of us.

"I like her voice," I said. "She'd be easier to market than someone wanting a comeback, is that right?" No need for subtlety.

"I have a fan base," Hargreaves said. She didn't look at me, just kept her eyes on McBain. "And I know how to get my songs played."

"Yes, you do," McBain said. "But I'm a manager, dear. I need more clients. I need to think of the future of my business."

Hargreaves bolted up from the chair. "And your bed? Is she in there, too?"

That was more like it.

"She's young," I said. "Too young for that."

Hargreaves didn't move for a second, her fists clenched and her back rigid with controlled emotion.

"I guess the pop industry likes young," I said. "Why don't you try to be more like Cher, do the Las Vegas thing."

Her control dissolved. "That's what you do when you're old." She spat the words at me.

I felt David take a step closer.

"Sorry, I shouldn't have said anything," I said. "I guess listening to Freyja made me wonder why your career isn't taking off again. Your husband does know talent when he sees it."

"Get out," she screamed. "All of you!"

I knew we'd see the action on Rory's recording. We'd hear it through the transmitter he'd put in our headphones if we left a set here. But I couldn't leave her alone to cool off.

"Mr. McBain?" David asked. "Should we go?"

I liked David's approach. Now McBain could tell us to stay, or mention the message, or do anything that would stop Hargreaves from sending us out.

"I think we should go," McBain said as if he'd been included in the order to leave.

"Not you," Hargreaves said. "Them. We need to talk about your new little protégé."

David didn't move, and I let him take the lead. It wasn't time to use my specials skills to provoke.

"Fine," McBain said. "We might as well just hash it out. We'll finish the session in five minutes."

"You'll go back to the session when I've had my say." Cecilie Hargreaves poked her husband in the shoulder to punctuate her sentence.

Chapter 46

David took my arm and I didn't want to put up a fight and distract Hargreaves or McBain. When we were outside, he let go and led me over to the other door to the studio. "We can observe from there," he said, pointing.

The room was empty. Freyja must have been with Luke, or just gone. The studio was well lit, and I didn't understand how we could watch them without being seen.

"We're in a blind spot," David said. "When Freyja came into the room, we didn't notice her right away. If we stand just inside the door, we won't be seen, but we'll have a clear view of them."

Voices rose in the booth. I put my headphones on and heard Hargreaves swearing at McBain. "Okay, let's try it out," I said.

"I'll stay out here," Rory said. "I can see them on my iPad. The video is streaming from the cameras. I'll just be in the way if I join you."

"Just stand back in case we need to run into the booth and break things up," David said.

We stepped into the studio and now I could see the two

combatants as well. They were both red faced with anger. The escalation in the few moments we'd been outside amazed me. McBain stood near the door like he was ready to flee. Hargreaves stood only inches away, yelling at him.

"You are my husband," she yelled. "Leave that skinny, talentless bitch alone."

"You can't order me around anymore," McBain said. "I know too much."

"Then you know how far I'll go to stop you." Her voice barely above a whisper now. The change from full on parade sergeant to quiet was chilling. "You know what I can do."

I took a step toward the door.

David touched my arm. "Not yet. They can still make something up to explain all that."

"You think McBain will? He knows we're recording."

"If he's mad enough, he won't think."

"He looks more scared," I said.

McBain hadn't responded to Hargreaves' threat. And I was wrong, now he looked calm. He took a step toward Hargreaves.

"Just how much longer do you think you can keep solving problems that way?" he asked. "Eventually you won't be able to hide it from the cops."

"They haven't found out yet," she said. "If I tell them you forced me to do anything you accuse me of, you'll lose everything."

"You won't tell them because there's nothing to tell. I'm innocent," McBain said. He pushed her away and turned to the door. "Let's find out what happens."

Hargreaves stumbled but then recovered. She reached into her purse and pulled out a collapsible baton. She extended it and swung at McBain, missing his head, but getting his shoulder.

He spun and grabbed for the baton. "That was a mistake, Cecilie. Did you forget who's outside?"

She jerked away and swung again.

David grabbed me into the hall and started for the sound booth door.

Hargreaves hit McBain on the temple and he went down.

I followed David into the room, and he read Hargreaves her rights.

"What are you arresting me for?" she asked, like she hadn't just knocked her husband out.

"We'll start with GBH and work from there," David said. "Hold out your hands."

"I will not let you handcuff me," Hargreaves said. She pulled her hands behind her. "My fans will crucify you."

"We don't care about your fans," I said. I knelt and checked McBain's pulse. "We need an ambulance."

"On the way," Rory said from the door.

David was still holding out the handcuffs. I reached for Hargreaves, trying to pull her arm so her hand would come forward. She wrenched it from my grasp.

"Just accept that you're coming with us," David said. "I don't want to bring in an armed force to finish this."

"No. Self-defense. He was going to hit me."

"We saw it all," I said.

Then Paul Grewal walked through the door. All in black with a bulletproof vest and a gun in a holster. I almost surrendered myself.

"Resisting arrest?" he asked. Like he didn't know.

"No need for tear gas," David said. "She'll come along."

The cop humor seemed out of place, and yet somehow perfect. I stepped out of the way because I didn't have the authority to arrest anyone.

McBain groaned on the floor but didn't move. Hargreaves tried to avoid the handcuffs, but between David and Paul, she had no hope. I heard Rory speaking in the background, telling Luke and Freyja to go back to the kitchen. But there were no other sounds. Grewal had left the rest of his team outside.

"Ma'am, I need you to cooperate," David said. He stood behind Hargreaves. He touched her arm. "Put your hands forward. It will hurt a lot more if you make us cuff you behind."

Why didn't he just do that? As long as she was unrestrained, she was dangerous.

Hargreaves became rigid, like a two-year-old in full tantrum. If they forced her into the cuffs, she'd be hurt, and no one wanted the trouble that would come from that.

She turned her head back and forth like she was denying them, but I knew she was looking for an exit. And there was one. The door from the booth to the studio only a step away. I didn't know if David had forgotten it, but he was focused on getting the cuffs on her. Grewal was watching the action, ready to move in if things went wrong.

I slipped out into the corridor and ran to the door into the recording space. I asked Rory to keep the door closed until we told him otherwise. He leaned against it as I shut it behind me.

My plan was to run across the studio and close off her exit. But she must have moved as soon as I left. I watched as she braced a chair under the handle of the other door. It wouldn't stop David or Paul, but it would give her some time.

Through the glass, I saw David kicking the door. Grewal said something into the walkie talkie on his shoulder.

Hargreaves saw me. "Get the fuck out of my way."

I took a step toward her. The equipment in the room made it impossible for her to get a clear run. "Just accept it," I said. "You are going down."

"I have good lawyers and a lot of money." As she spoke, Hargreaves sidestepped a drum set and a music stand. "It should have been you at Lumberman's Arch, not the cop."

"Did you kill all of them?" I moved to block her.

David kept kicking at the door, but Grewal had disappeared.

"I'm not going to tell you anything," she said.

Apparently, she didn't think mentioning the attack told me something.

All I had to do was keep her here until Paul got to Rory and came through the door. He should have done that by now.

Hargreaves picked up an electric cord from the floor. She threw it at me, but it didn't come close. I ducked anyway, damn instincts.

A drumstick came next, then a loose microphone. She was a bad shot and I managed to avoid being hit, but she was herding me to the side. Now she was almost past me, but across the room from the door. I changed position.

She bent and pulled at another cord on the floor.

I was standing on the other end of it. I landed on my ass.

She ran toward me as I tried to stand.

She stepped on my hand; agony shot from my fingers to my shoulder.

I rolled and got to my knees.

I heard the door crack open.

Hargreaves rushed past me.

I grabbed her. With my injured hand. The pain almost knocked me out.

Hargreaves fell flat on her face. She screamed and rolled over. Blood poured from her nose.

"Freeze." The words came from both sides of me. David had made it through the door, and Grewal was finally in the room.

I cradled my hand and watched as they handcuffed Hargreaves. She was still screaming as Grewal handed her to another officer with instructions to see the doctor at booking.

"What took you so long?" I asked, the pain in my hand making me sob the first word.

"It was ten seconds," Grewal said. "I thought Anchor had you."

David helped me up. "You were great," he said and then looked at my hand. "I think maybe you broke a finger or two."

"Next time maybe rescue me faster," I said by way of a thank you.

"Next time don't go rushing off to fight a maniac by yourself," David said. "Let's get you to emergency."

The ER could be hours. "I want to be there for the interview."

"She's already asked for a lawyer," David said. "We have time."

He wrapped his arm around me and led me to the door.

Rory grinned and focused his camera on me. "Dude! That was epic."

Chapter 47

It took three hours. I needed x-rays to learn that my ring and baby fingers were broken. I had a splint that I couldn't get wet, an appointment for a follow-up in a week, and assurances that I'd probably regain the use in four to six weeks.

I didn't take the painkillers. I'm not a hero or a masochist. I just didn't want to be fuzzy when I listened to the interview.

Leigh was in the observation room when I arrived. Rory and Kardozian were there too, but they stood in the back. "Good work, Deacon," Kardozian said.

"Val says stop getting yourself in the hospital," Rory said.

Her version of 'get better soon'. "Thanks. What happened while I was out?"

"Nothing," Leigh said. "McBain is in the hospital under guard in case his wife tries something. He'll be here in the morning to make a statement. Hargreaves has been seen by the doctor. Good work on her nose, by the way.

She's been yelling at her lawyer since he arrived. I expect we'll be called in soon."

"They let me put my camera in the room," Rory said. "This is going to win awards."

Kardozian chuckled. "Don't forget that we have to approve whatever you produce."

"I'm planning to interview everyone who gave approval, so they can tell the audience their take on it." Rory leaned against the back wall. "It should help them say yes."

I guessed Val had something to do with that decision. She had a knack for getting the answer she wanted.

The door opened in the interview room. Paul and David walked in, sat down and placed a thick file on the table.

"My client is willing to answer your questions," the lawyer said. "She reserves the right to stay silent if she deems anything too personal."

That sounded weird to me. Did she get the right to decide which questions to answer?

"She does have the right to remain silent, Charity," Leigh said like she read my mind. "If she starts talking, it will be hard for her to stop."

"We have a number of questions," David said. "Let's start with the attack on Detective Andrews."

"I didn't want to do that," Hargreaves said. "Ernie, my husband, made me do it. He threatened to hurt me."

That was a bit too easy.

"So, you did attack her at Lumberman's Arch?" David asked.

"Yes. I have bruises on my stomach and hips from when her partner attacked me."

"We'll leave that for now," David said.

"But I need to tell you how Ernie bullied me into all of this," she said.

"We'll decide what we need to know," Paul Grewal said.

"Do any of these names mean anything to you?" David referred to a list on the table. "Helena Tripton, death by poisoning, Jackson Tripton, death by poisoning, Alex Sandhu, stabbed to death, Mary Copp, victim of attempted murder, Ronald Waters, suspicious overdose death, Victoria LaSalle, murdered."

"Are they fans?"

He passed her the pictures one at a time. "Anything now?"

"These people are all dead."

"Yes," he said. "You don't recognize any of them?"

"No."

David picked out two photos. "Your husband, Jackson Tripton. His sister, Helena."

"I meant none of the others."

I was getting a headache. I don't know what I was expecting, but this game where she lied openly for hours wasn't it.

"They'll keep going until she makes a mistake. That was the first one, not knowing the victims," Leigh said.

I knew I wouldn't be able to stick through hours of this. "When will they press charges?"

"We'll hold her until after we've talked to McBain," Kardozian said. "You should both get some rest and come back to observe his interview."

"Can we get more evidence now that we know she's the killer?" I tried not to let the 'I told you so' leak into my tone.

"Yes, there'll be something," Leigh said. "Go home. I'll call you if anything breaks. You can watch the recording."

The pain in my fingers was throbbing through my whole body. If I could sleep, it would be better to be here when McBain gave us the real answers.

"Can I get a ride home?"

Kardozian called down to the front desk and asked them to arrange for a cruiser.

Chapter 48

A solid night's sleep did wonders. Pain still throbbed in my hand, but my mind was clearer. Yesterday's fogginess probably had more to do with the trauma of the break than the actual injury.

David picked me up at seven, which might have been sweet, but Leigh already sat in the car when I got there. He was on invalid duty.

"We got Hargreaves," he said. "She started screwing up after a couple of hours. Her lawyer tried to get her to stop talking, but nothing worked."

"How long did it take?" I asked. Hargreaves deserved to spend time being grilled given what she'd done to me and Leigh.

"Five hours," he said. "We gave her the requisite breaks, but eventually she just started bragging."

"LaSalle?" Leigh asked.

"Yep, and the new case, the witness, and Mary Copp," David said. "Ian found the connection to the other cases. It seemed to make the difference."

"Helena?" I asked.

"She says McBain did that one. He changed his name when he came to Vancouver. Used to be Oliver Frankston. We'll need to confirm that. She tried to blame everything on him after we told her he was in a coma, too."

"You lied?"

"We can do that."

"Althea will be happy. She suspected him from the start but didn't know about the name change. If we had a picture of McBain on us, the case would have been over sooner."

"Calgary is making noise for us to release him to their custody," David said, pulling into the parking lot. "You'll be in the observation room, Charity."

"Fine." I didn't need to be asking questions.

"Leigh, we got the okay to let you interview with Paul."

"What about you?" Leigh asked. "You were on our cases long enough to merit the interview, let alone on the LaSalle case."

"One from each team," he said, opening the door for me. "There's no way Paul was going to delegate it."

Getting us settled with Rory and Kardozian in the room took a while. They didn't bring McBain in until around ten. Rory spent the time testing his equipment. The rest of us worked out and agreed on the questions. This time, David and I were wired in, so we could prompt Leigh or Paul if we thought of something.

"I want to be clear, Charity, don't interrupt on a whim or an idea. Only something critical," Kardozian said. "Leave any new information to me."

"Yes, ma'am." I smiled and touched the lapel microphone. "I'll be good."

"Good thing we have it on record," she said.

I didn't respond because a uniformed officer escorted McBain into the room. He was joined by the same lawyer who'd represented Hargreaves.

"Isn't that conflict of interest or something?" I asked.

"She fired him," David said.

Chapter 49

Everything was much calmer than yesterday. McBain looked defeated, the bandage on his head adding to the effect. Had they already told him his wife threw him under the bus?

"Ernest McBain, this interview is to gather details on the crimes you've been charged with; four counts of murder, two of abetting Grievous Bodily Harm, and one of committing the same offense."

"My client has been advised of the charges," the lawyer said.

"Has he been advised that his wife accused him of aiding in or committing eight murders?" Paul Grewal was taking the lead.

Eight? What had I missed?

Leigh sat back and stared at McBain. He kept flicking a glance at her while trying to stay focused on Paul.

"You're lying." He licked his lips. "She would never do that to me."

Paul placed what looked like a mobile phone on the

table. He tapped the screen and Hargreaves' voice came out.

It must have been toward the end of her interview. She was listing the victims and saying who did the planning and who did the killing. They'd worked as a team the whole time; she gave us more names than were in the official cases.

Paul stopped the playback and waited.

McBain looked at his lawyer who gave him no help. He looked at Leigh. "How did you make her say those words? She wouldn't have..."

"Why did you kill Alex Sandhu?" Leigh asked.

"That reporter was getting close. Cecilie told me after she did it. A random killing would break any pattern LaSalle saw."

"So, simply because she could?" Leigh leaned forward, protecting her shoulder with the other hand. "And Mary Copp? Did you make the shrine?"

I saw what they were doing. McBain was off kilter from hearing Hargreaves confess. Leigh assumed he would answer, so she was getting the holes in our investigation filled.

"She was stalking Cecilie," he said. "We went to her house. Cecilie said it was only to talk to her, but she showed us that room. It gave me the creeps."

"So, you tried to kill her?" Paul asked.

"No, Cecilie did," McBain said. "She said we could point to the crazy woman if we ever got arrested. All it would take is a few more photos to link everyone we killed to Copp."

"But she didn't die," Leigh said.

"Yeah, that was a problem. Cecilie went to the hospital to try to finish what I'd screwed up. That reporter was there. They fought, at least that's what Cecilie told me. It was an accident."

"Do you believe her?" Leigh asked.

"I did," McBain said. "Maybe now, no."

"This is all very interesting," Lawyer guy said. "What exactly are you charging my client with? Some vague murder or helping to murder won't cut it in court. And if it's because he didn't report a crime...well, I can argue that down to time served."

"Just cleaning up the details," Leigh said.

Lawyer guy looked at Ernie. "Then, I'll ask you to charge my client or let him go."

I thought it was a bit over the top, and if Hargreaves had listened to him, she might not be facing all the charges.

"It's a bargaining ploy," David said. "He knows McBain isn't walking out."

Leigh looked at Paul, who shrugged.

"There might be something," Paul said. "You could save us some time sorting it out by telling us everything. We can talk to The Crown about a chance for parole."

"Give us a minute," Lawyer guy said.

Leigh and Paul left the interrogation room and turned the sound off. David and Kardozian left the observation room but said Rory and I could stay since we weren't officers of the law.

"What if he attacks the lawyer?" I asked.

"There's nothing for him to use, and he's handcuffed," David said.

We didn't have much of a wait. The lawyer stood and opened the door after only a few minutes, calling Leigh and Paul back in.

Kardozian and David rejoined us, and the show started again.

"My client has evidence that will ensure Ms. Hargreaves is found guilty," Lawyer guy said. "You will have no trouble understanding how she manipulated him when you see it. We need to hear from The Crown Prosecutor before we continue."

"On her way," Leigh said.

"Then we'll wait."

McBain put his arms on the table and laid his head on them. I swear I heard him crying.

"How long before she gets here?" I asked.

"She's downstairs right now," David said. "We expected something like this. We want to let him stew. If McBain has enough time, we won't have to make a great deal, just something."

They waited an hour, then a woman in a dark suit joined them. She carried an air of boredom, like she negotiated with murderers every day. Like whatever they had to bargain with wouldn't be enough.

"This is Crown Prosecutor Ireland," Leigh said. She didn't introduce anyone else.

"All I can offer is some possibility of parole. Your client will serve serious time even as an accomplice after the fact. I don't care how afraid of his wife he was."

"Parole in?" Lawyer asked.

"Standard twenty-five years." Ireland didn't leave room for argument.

"My client will be in his eighties," Lawyer said.

"At least he'll be out of prison," Ireland said.

"It's enough," McBain muttered. "I'm not getting away with this, so it will be enough."

"Contingent on your information being useful." Ireland crossed her arms.

"In my office. The top drawer of my credenza. Secret panel in the back. Photos of Cecilie in the act."

"Will that be enough?" I asked. "Pictures can be altered."

"We have specialists to prove they are originals," Kardozian said. "Relax, Charity, we won't screw this up without you."

"Does that mean you'll wait for me before you screw it up?"

Kardozian laughed.

Chapter 50

It turned out that McBain wasn't the only one with a trophy collection. We didn't even have to give Hargreaves a deal to get it. Kardozian got us a search warrant so we weren't restricted to the top drawer of the credenza. Now that we knew about secret drawers, it took all of half an hour to find where she'd stashed videos of McBain; they proved he was more than just a tool. He'd killed Helena and changed his name when he left Calgary just like Cecilie said. No deal for him.

We still had paperwork, but by the end of the day, we were ready to celebrate.

"Dinner?" David asked. "We should all go for a drink at least."

AN HOUR LATER, Leigh, David, Rory, Val, and I crowded around a table at The Sandbar restaurant on Granville Island. Wine glasses half full, appetizers in the middle for sharing and me feeling a little sad.

It was all over. I needed to figure out what to fill my time with starting tomorrow.

"David and I are partners, now," Leigh said.

"Great," I said.

"We might see more of you," David said.

I sipped my wine to avoid answering his comment. We were here to celebrate closing the case, not...whatever this was.

"What are you going to do?" Val asked in her usual 'let's get on with it' attitude. "Matthieu and Lu are going to be gone for a long time."

"Thanks for caring," I said. "I'll start looking for clients. I'm sure someone needs me."

"Maybe take a few days to recover?" David nodded toward my bandaged hand.

"I'll look for clients who aren't out to kill me."

"Are there any?" He laughed. "Sorry, that was probably too soon, right?"

I couldn't stifle my grin. "If you wait for when it's not too soon, you might never make the joke."

"We'll give you a reference," Leigh said. "Excellent at annoying people until they confess to crimes."

"Very funny." I took a sip of wine. "Maybe I should take a vacation."

"Maybe you should go on a date," Val said.

My cheeks burned. "Too personal." *And not at all subtle.*

David grinned at me. "I'm still willing to risk going on a date."

"You could do worse," Leigh said.

It was the most uncomfortable set up I'd ever suffered. David was nice, and good looking, and funny, and he'd seen me at my snarkiest. And it was time I stopped mourning the loss of my relationship with Jake. And I could always say the wine and painkillers made me more susceptible to suggestion.

"Let's say I agree," I said. "What kind of date would we go on?"

"I'm thinking a movie, dinner, maybe a walk along the seawall?"

"This one, right?" The seawall in Stanley Park felt a little too dangerous after this case.

"I thought you'd balk at walking," David said. "Yes, this one. As far as I know, none of us has been attacked around here."

"Pick me up tomorrow around seven," I said.

Want More?

When Charity investigates a wandering spouse, the last thing she expects to find is a mob boss with intent to murder. Use the QR code to grab your copy of PRIDE.

If you enjoyed reading Dreams, please consider helping other readers to find the story by leaving a review.

Free eBook

Claim your copy of Buying Into Death when you use the QR code to sign up for my newsletter and follow Charity as she solves her fastest case yet!

Also by P A Wilson

For more books by P A Wilson

Use the QR code below or go to pawilson.ca

About the Author

Perry Wilson is a Canadian author based in Vancouver, BC who has big ideas and an itch to tell stories. Having spent some time on university, a career, and life in general, she returned to writing in 2008 and hasn't looked back since (well, maybe a little, but only while parallel parking).

She is a member of the Vancouver Writers Social Group, The Royal City Literary Arts Society, and The Surrey Writing Workshop. Perry has self-published several novels. She writes the Madeline Journeys, a fantasy series about a high-powered lawyer who finds herself trapped in a magical world, the Quinn Larson Quests, which follows the adventures of a wizard named Quinn who must contend with volatile fae in the heart of Vancouver, and the Charity Deacon Investigations, a mystery thriller series about a private eye who tends to fall into serious trouble with her cases, and The Riverton Romances, a series based in a small town in Oregon, one of her favorite states. Her stand-alone novels are Breaking the Bonds, Closing the Circle, and The Dragon at The Edge of The Map.

For more information
www.pawilson.ca
pawilson@pawilson.ca

Acknowledgments

People think that the process of writing is solitary. That's not the case for me. I have help from so many people it would be hard to acknowledge everyone, but I'll give it a try.

The support and inspiration I get from my writer's groups is incalculable. The Vancouver Writers Social Group opens my mind to other ways of telling a story. The Royal City Literary Arts Society gives me the opportunity to meet and share with other writers who have more knowledge than I do. The Other 11 Months group is where I learn about getting the words on the page. And my critique group who helps me find the best parts of the story I want to tell. Thanks to all of the members of these great groups.

Last of all, but definitely a huge part of the process, my beta readers. These are the people who love stories and are willing, and more than able, to tell me if my finished story is ready for you, my readers.